# Metal Spikes III

Warren Haskin

# Metal Spikes III

Warren Haskin

Published By
**Positive Imaging, LLC**
bill@positive-imaging.com



ISBN   9781951776336

# Praise for Metal Spikes Series

Billy Tankersly is back!  We've all been waiting to
see what it would be like to live as a big leaguer and
Warren doesn't disappoint.  This book focuses more
on the daily life of a kid-turned-baseball star and the
way a positive outlook and high-expectations can
change your world and the people around you.  Billy
continues to look to his mentors for inspiration and
shows what can happen when you open yourself to
the possibilities of a Great Attitude.  Warren knocks
another one out of the park.  Can't wait for the next
book in the series. **Bill Hagara**

I don't remember a fictional baseball story about a
young man, growing up to play professional baseball
before.  I'm sure there has been one that I just don't
remember, but Metal Spikes I & II are fascinating
books, by what I suspect is an up and coming author.
**Fred Troutman, Houston, Tx.**

"Another great (and more streamlined) read from Mr.
Haskin - full of life lessons.  I love all the play-by-
plays and feel as if I'm sitting in the stands for each
game.  All parents need to hand this book to their
youngsters, whatever their aspirations."
**Catherine Athearn**

# Contents

# DEDICATION

This book is dedicated to BaseBallManager.com (BBM), the best baseball game on the Internet ever! I've played it for 31 straight years, and have finally traded for, or picked up among the Free Agents, ALL KC Royals. It's not a game for the faint of heart as you have to make lineup changes every day, 162 days a year, depending on who is pitching against you. For a fanatic baseball fan....BBM is the ultimate.

# FOREWARD

**Book One** of the three-book series follows Billy Tankersly and his best friend, Bobby Bonds, from age 9 to age 16. Billy has a goal to break Ricky Henderson's Stolen Base Record in Major League Baseball. Bobby is a homerun hitter growing up. The two boys get separated at age 13 when Bobby's dad finds a better job in Austin, Texas. Both boys get on traveling baseball teams in their respective cities and remain close friends in constant contact, comparing their goals and successes as they grow up. Billy has a mentor, Mr. Booker, who is in the Baseball Hall of Fame. As Billy grows, with instructions from Mr. Booker, he gets faster and faster. He realizes he must set one goal at a time, and his first goal is getting drafted by his hometown KC Royals.

**Book Two** is about Billy's minor league struggles. Once he begins to grasp his mental game, he realizes that his coaches up to this point have given him all the information needed to succeed. Billy starts applying the attitude necessary to build up his stolen base totals in the minors. The unexpected happens when the starting Royals shortstop gets injured. Billy has been promoted to the Royals AAA team, the Omaha Storm Chasers. Once Skip had been injured, The Royals Management decide to let their rising star test the waters of Major League baseball. Once the season is over, Billy questions if he'll get to play with the Royals the next year, since Skip Anderson, the regular SS, will be healthy.

**Book Three** has Billy and Bobby making it to the major leagues. Will Billy break Ricky Henderson's stolen base record?  What happens next is in this book. Enjoy!!!  ☺

# <u>1</u>

## A Surprise In Des Moines

Billy suited up in his Storm Chaser uniform.  Coach Keller explained why Billy had been sent down.  Like Billy suspected, it was because the Royals had to stick with their high-paying shortstop, Skip Anderson.  He told Billy that he would more than likely be the first player called up if there was an injury, but the Royals did not want Billy to be sitting on the bench every day.

"Hey, Billy," Bobby shouted from across the diamond.  Throw me a low one so I can practice scooping it up."

Bobby was now playing 1B for the Storm Chasers and was told by the Royals that there was a chance he could be called up this year.  The Royals had been spending money on an Urban Baseball Camp for African American's because of the fall-off in black boys coming to baseball.  It seemed most African Americans were playing more basketball and football rather than baseball.  With Bobby being the only African American close to being ready for the big time in the Royals minor leagues, they were anxious to see Bobby have a good year where they could promote him as soon as he was ready.

Both young men were looked upon by the Royals as part of the future of the franchise.  Mack had been sent down too, and Billy knew the Royals were looking at him as their future at 2B.

"Maybe all three of them would be playing on the Royals by the end of the year," Billy thought as he tossed one low throw after another toward Bobby at 1B in their first practice session since arriving in Omaha.

The Storm Chasers would be playing their first game against the Iowa Cubs, the Triple A club of the Chicago Cubs. Their opening series was to be played at Principal Stadium in Des Moines day after tomorrow. Today, the Storm Chasers were playing against the University of Nebraska in a warmup game. It was a seven-inning exhibition game that the Storm Chasers barely won. It came down to the last of the 7th and Pete Lorrenze, the team's centerfielder, hit a sacrifice fly to score Terrace Moore, who was to be the right fielder for the team this year. Both players were coming up from Double A, so they were pretty excited. The "old-timers" on the team were excited for them.

After the game, the players boarded the team bus to go from Omaha to Des Moines, which was only an hour from Omaha. Billy and Bobby were sitting next to each other and talked about Spring Training, about the coming year, and of course, Emma.

"Bobby, I've never really thanked you for not asking Emma out," Billy started, realizing he and Bobby had not talked about Emma since arriving in Surprise, Arizona for Spring Training or here in Omaha.

"What was the point?" Bobby stated. All she did when we were together was talk about you."

"Bobby," Billy laughed. "She told me that when the two of you were together, all you did was talk about me."

"You are the one who told me not to ask her out," Bobby said with a frown on his face.

Billy laughed at his best friend.

"Would you have asked her out if I'd not said anything?" Billy asked.

"Is Austin the Capital of Texas?" Bobby laughed. "Heck, yes, I would have.  She is the most beautiful girl I've ever met, and she is a baseball fan."

"Yep, she is both," Billy said, thinking about Emma now and not their upcoming season opener.

"I haven't had time to tell you, Bobby, but I flew to Lexington before going to Spring Training, and we had our first date," Billy was now excited to be talking about Emma again.  He'd called her after getting the news that he was being sent down to Omaha.  She told him to keep his mind on baseball because she wanted to watch him steal his 1,407th base some year in the future.

"Bobby, I think I'm in love with Emma," Billy finally told his best friend.

"Billy?" Bobby asked, in a serious mood because he had not heard about Billy dating Emma until now, at least not from Billy.

"We spent a lot of time talking, about baseball, you, fishing," Billy started.

"Fishing?" Bobby interrupted.

Billy told Bobby about renting the boat, fishing all day, and getting back to the dock so late that the owner of the boat had already left.  He shared with his best friend about sitting in the boat with Emma, thinking they might be there all night.

"That was the first time I'd kissed her, Bobby," Billy started, definitely thinking more about Emma than his upcoming game.

"Billy, do not let a girl get in the way of you breaking Ricky's record," Bobby warned.

"Yeah, I hear you, buddy," Billy said, still thinking about Emma.

The bus arrived in Des Moines in time for dinner. As they exited the bus, Billy saw her, standing off on the curb. He had to do a double-take to make sure that it was Emma.

"Bobby, Emma is here," he shouted to his best bud.

Bobby laughed.

Billy went running over to Emma, lifting her and swinging her around. He didn't care what the other players thought.

"What are you doing here?" Billy asked in disbelief that she was here.

"Well, your best friend called me and asked if I could drive up from Lexington to see you guys in your first game," she answered.

"Bobby did that?" he asked, stunned.

Bobby was now by their side, hugging Emma, thanking her for coming.

Billy was confused. What was his best friend giving Emma a hug when he'd just told him that he thought he was in love with this girl?

"Emma, you will be happy to know that all during Spring Training, Billy did not mention your name once," Bobby started.

Billy wondered, "What exactly is going on here?"

She hugged Billy again and kissed him in front of Bobby and the few team members who had not gone into the hotel yet.

"Billy, I couldn't help myself. I texted Bobby during Spring Training to ask how you were doing,"

Emma started explaining. We texted back and forth several times, and I had to tell Bobby about our first kiss."

"What?" Billy looked at Bobby as he was talking. "You mean you let me talk about Emma, telling you about our first kiss when you already knew.

Bobby laughed louder than Billy had ever heard him laugh.

"You have no idea how hard it was to keep a straight face as you were telling me," Bobby cackled.

The three walked arm in arm into the restaurant, where the rest of the team was. As they entered, everyone stood and started clapping. Billy was stunned. Did the entire team know?

"Yes, I told everyone about Emma showing up tonight, and how surprised you'd be, and asked them all to not mention it to you," Bobby told his best friend.

After dinner, the three of them talked a while before Bobby said, "Hey kids, it's time Billy and I get to bed. We've got a game tomorrow," Bobby said in a joking way, but also serious.

Billy walked Emma to her room and then settled down in his room, thinking about Emma and then reminding himself that breaking Ricky's record was more important than anything else.

He dozed off to sleep thinking about getting three hits in the season opener tomorrow and making the Royals call him up sooner than they had imagined, and maybe marrying Emma along the way.

# 2

## First Game Of The Season

Billy's first thought as he saw the lineup card with him batting third and Bobby cleanup, was how similar it seemed to their first game together on the Rockets when they were both nine years old.

Mack was leading off with Arturo Cruz, playing centerfield, hitting second. Billy had his bat in his hand as the first pitch was thrown to Mack.

"Ball one," bellowed the umpire, who Billy remembered from last year.

One the next pitch, Mack hit a ground ball between SS and 3B, and no one was able to reach it.

"Way to start the season, Mack," yelled Billy getting ready to step into the on deck circle, still wishing he was in the leadoff spot and wanting to steal. He looked up into the crowd to see if he could find Emma. Before he could spot her, Arturo hit a line drive to left field that was walloped,  and Mack had to stop at 2B. Billy forgot about Emma. His only thought, "Get a hit to drive in the first run of the season."

He watched the first pitch, a fastball, hit the outside corner of the plate. He didn't even need to hear the umpire signaling the pitch was a strike.

He turned around, remembering Art Brown, the umpire, who was the first person in a game to congratulate him last year after being promoted to the Storm Chasers. "Hey ump, you know that was a ball," he laughed, stepping out of the box.

"Don't give me any trouble, hotshot," Art Brown returned the banter.

With two strikes on him, Billy choked up about ½ inch on the bat.  He was expecting a curve, and as he watched the spin from the pitcher's hand, he knew he'd guessed right. He swung hard and ended up hitting a slug bunt that bounced high in the air, giving him enough time to beat the throw to first base.

Now the bases were loaded for Bobby.  Billy had not seen Bobby play in a real game, outside of the exhibition game against the University of Nebraska, since the travel squad went to Austin for a tournament.  He'd seen enough of his power in Spring Training to know the pitcher better not give Bobby the same pitch he threw to him.  He did, and Bobby hit the first pitch over the left-field wall by 30 feet.  Bobby had just hit his first Grand Slam HR in a Storm Chaser uniform.

As Bobby rounded the bases, Mack, Arturo, and Billy all waited at the plate to congratulate Bobby. The Storm Chasers led 4-0, and the Cubs pitcher had not gotten a single out.  The Cubs pitching coach walked to the mound to try to steady Goose Tyson, the starting pitcher.  Tyson was up in the big leagues about the same amount of time as Billy last year, so Billy knew this was not the usual Goose Tyson.

After the pitching coach visited the mound, Goose settled down and struck out the next three Omaha hitters.

Billy and the rest of the Storm Chasers took the field in the bottom of the first.  It was fun playing with Bobby again, especially after seeing his best friend hit one so far out of the park that Tyson didn't even turn around to watch it.  He knew from the sound of the bat hitting the ball that he'd never see that ball again.  He forgot that the Storm Chasers bullpen was behind the fence, and after the game, won by the Storm Chases, 5-1, the relievers who had been in the bullpen gave Bobby his first professional Grand Slam baseball.  They seemed to be more excited about giving Bobby the ball than he was in hitting it.

"It is going to be a fun year, Billy thought," hoping he, Mack and Bobby would be called up to the Royals by the time the All-Star break occurred, but for now, Billy was a Storm Chaser, and he knew what he had to do to get called up.  Steal bases.

The Storm Chasers won all three games of the series. They were now headed to New Orleans, where they would play the Baby Cakes, who had won the Pacific Coast Division last year.

Emma only stayed for the first game of the series, so Billy was able to devote 100% to baseball as they got on the bus to New Orleans.  Bobby turned to Billy on the bus ride, asking, "Do you have any idea why they are called the Baby Cakes.....that's pretty strange."

"Now that you asked, the Baby Cakes were originally the Zephyrs, but after 23 years, the fans asked the Owners to change the name.  President Lou Schwechheimer of the team said the name was a "tribute to the Mardi Gras king cakes," answered Billy.

"That still is a strange name," Bobby replied, almost laughing at it.  Then he wondered how many other teams came to New Orleans laughing about the name of the team they were to play.

It was a long trip from Des Moines to New Orleans, something like 12 hours plus, so most of the players tried to sleep. At least the bus ride wasn't as bad as the bus in Lexington. Billy decided that was a memory he'd keep forever, as an affirmation to reach the majors fast.

Because of the long road trip, the next day was an off-day, but the bus wouldn't even get into New Orleans until something like 4:00 AM, so most of the players hit their beds as soon as they arrived,

Billy and Bobby were no different. Once they checked into the motel outside of the French Quarter, they both went straight to bed. Billy was back to sleeping with his bat.

# <u>3</u>

## New Orleans Series

Exploring New Orleans the next day opened their eyes to the history of the city as they walked around, seeing the French Architecture from the 1700s. Occupied by the French and Spanish from the 17th century until the Louisiana Purchase in 1803 for pennies an acre, New Orleans still maintained a European feel. It changed since 1803 but still has the original buildings from that period.

"How do you know all this, Billy?" Bobby asked. Billy laughed and said he read about it in a brochure in their room before going to sleep. They both laughed and gazed at the buildings all around the French Quarter. They'd been told to hit the Café Du Monde for their fresh, soft beignets. "What in the world is a beignet?" Bobby asked.

"A beignet is like a Chinese donut, but even more important, it's been an iconic staple for all those years," Billy replied.

"How in the world do you know all this stuff, Billy?" Bobby asked.

"Have you ever heard of searching for things on the Internet, Bobby?" Billy laughed. But in this case, it also was in the brochure in our hotel room," Billy laughed even harder.

The team was meeting at the New Orleans ballpark at 4:00 PM to take batting and infield practice. For some reason, Billy didn't do good in the batting cage, but his fielding was like normal, far superior to any other SS in Triple A; at least that was what he read in a New Orleans paper he picked up that afternoon. He was a little worried about why he didn't see the ball well in batting practice.

The game started the next day at promptly 1:00 PM, with the Storm Chasers up first as the visiting team. Mack and Arturo batted first and second with Billy and Bobby hitting third and fourth. Mack took the first two pitches for strikes and then watched a curveball break more than any curve Billy had ever seen break.....it was like it started at head level on the outside of the plate and then straight down to finish below Mack's knees on the inside of the plate. The Ump called "Strike Three." Mack was amazed. He couldn't believe that the ball was really over the plate. Billy was still in the dugout, but he saw what that ball did and wanted to be ready for it, if the New Orleans pitcher, Zack Issuse, threw it to him.

Arturo didn't fare much better. He fouled off two straight fastballs, and Billy yelled, warning him to watch out for Issuse's curve. Sure enough, he did the same thing to Arturo that he did to Mack. Once again, the umpire bellowed out, "Strike Three." Arturo turned around to argue, but instead of arguing, he asked the umpire, "was that a strike as it crossed the plate?" The umpire just smiled back at him and shook his head up and down.

Billy was ready. He figured Issuse would start off with a couple of fastballs, probably outside or inside non-hittable, and then come in with that curve. Billy was determined to watch the spin on the ball as it left Issuse's hand. He was surprised because he could tell from the spin that the New Orleans pitcher was starting him with his curve. Billy watched it on the inside of the plate and laid off it, knowing it was a "tease-pitch" to get Billy to swing. "Strike One," yelled the umpire. Billy was shocked. There was no way that was a strike. He didn't bother to turn and ask the ump as he saw Orturo do that and watched the umpire shake his head up and down. Billy expected a fastball on the second pitch since Issuse had started him with the curve, but once again, Billy saw the spin and swung, just getting a tip of it. "Foul Ball," said the umpire, almost congratulating Billy that he even tipped it. Now, it was a thinking game between the pitcher and Billy. Billy knew the pitcher was doing his best to set Billy up for a strikeout, but he didn't know whether to expect a fastball or another curve. He knew it was going to be a guessing game for both of them, trying to fool the other. It was a fastball, and Billy hit a sharp line drive directly at the right fielder. Three up, three down.

Butch Kelly was the starting pitcher for the Storm Chasers, and he also had a good curve, but nothing like what Issuse was throwing. The Baby Cakes got one man on, but on a ground ball to Mack's left, he did a 180 throwing to Billy at second, and Billy touched the base with his right foot while throwing to Bobby at 1st base for a Double Play.

The remaining innings went like the first with no score for the next six innings. In the last of the 7th, Butch gave up a HR to the Baby Cakes cleanup hitter, so going into the top of the 8th, the score was 1-0 with the Chasers trailing. Billy was first up, and after going 0-2, with one walk, he was hungry for a hit.

He noticed the third baseman was playing more toward the SS side. They must have known Billy was pretty much a pull hitter. After taking a mighty cut at the first pitch, he waited for either a curve or a changeup. Either way, he knew what he was going to do. It was a changeup, and Billy dropped a beautiful bunt down the third baseline and was easily safe at 1B on the throw.

The Storm Chaser manager was wasting no time going to Billy's strength......the steal sign was relayed from the dugout to the third base coach, and he, in turn, gave Billy the sign to steal on the first pitch. Issue, who was still in the game, threw to first to keep Billy from getting a good size lead. But, the instant his leg crossed the rubber, Billy was off for second base. "Safe" came the call from the infield umpire. Now, if Bobby could only get him in.

Bobby stepped back into the box, amazed at how fast Billy had gotten to second on the steal. The catcher threw a strike to the 2nd baseman covering, but it wasn't nearly soon enough to catch Billy. Bobby took a curve on the first pitch that bounced off to the right of the catcher. Billy was off. He slid into third, without the catcher even throwing to try to get him. It was ruled a "steal" by the official scorekeeper, so Billy had two steals in one inning.

Bobby hit a short fly ball to the centerfielder, and Billy was once again, off and running. He saw Christian Louis, the next batter, signaling for Billy to slide. He grabbed the corner of the plate as he slid past it, and the umpire had his arms spread, so Billy knew he was safe. It turned out to be the tying run, and the Chasers scored in the 9th on a long HR by Jackson Thade, the third baseman, and after the game was over, Bobby walked next to Billy. "I was shocked to see how fast you were on the bases today," Bobby said to Billy. "Well, if you had just hit the ball further, I wouldn't have had to run that fast," Billy jibbed his best friend. The two boys were just thankful they won the first game of the three game series.

The next two games were just the opposite of the low-scoring first game. The Baby Cakes won the second game 11-7. Billy was 0-4 and not at all happy with his hitting. Bobby had another HR that scored two of the seven runs but struck out in the 9th inning with men on 1st and 2nd. Neither boy was happy after the game. They discussed the Baby Cakes pitching staff, but went back to the hotel, disgusted with losing the game. The conversation was short and sweet as each grabbed a late dinner and hit the sack.

The third game was another low scoring game like the first game, but neither of the best friends even got a hit. The Baby Cakes won the game, 3-2. Billy was definitely in a slump. The bus ride was from New Orleans to Oklahoma City, where they were going to be playing the Dodgers in the Chickasaw Bricktown Ball Park. They had been in the AAA league since 1962, which surprised Billy as he was reading about the team, the stadium, and all he could learn. The Dodgers played in the Southern Division of the American Conference, while the Chasers were in the Northern Division. All that meant was they would not play each other but two more times all season. Since the Dodgers were leading the Southern Division with a 10-2 record, which was two more wins than the Chasers, they all knew they would have their hands full in winning the three game series.

As daunting as coming away with a series win looked, the Storm Chasers won all three games.

Bobby had two HR's and was now hitting .310, while Billy remained in his slump.  He only got one hit in the three games, and his average was below the Mendosa line, which meant he was hitting less than .200.

## <u>4</u>

## Emma Plays Hardball Too

Billy was happy the team was headed home and that they had one day off before the series started. The first of three teams to come to Omaha during the homestand was the Memphis Redbirds, followed by the Iowa Cubs and the Round Rock Express. The Cubs had a losing record, but the Redbirds and Express were hot after losing their first three games. Billy knew it would be an exciting homestand and that the stands would be full, cheering the team on. But he could not get his mind off his slump. It was starting to bother him as he'd never gone this long, with hits this far and few between.

His slump continued in the series against the Redbirds, and the Storm Chasers lost all three games. Billy only got one hit, but he did steal two bases because he walked one other time at the plate. His average sank even lower, while Bobby continued hitting HRs. He had two in the three games and now led the league with 8 HR's, and most of them were long HR's. Billy read in the newspaper that Bobby's last HR traveled 415 feet and left his bat at 108 mph.

With no off days during the homestand, Billy was in the batting cage more than ever. "What am I doing wrong?" he thought to himself. He even asked Bobby if he could see why he was in this month-long slump.

"Billy, I think you are trying too hard," Bobby answered. "I noticed in the last game; your head was looking toward first base when you stuck out."

"Maybe I'm trying to hit more HR's than you," Billy laughed, but it was a forced laugh. He did take Bobby's observation and made sure in the batting cages; he kept his eye on the ball as he hit.

In the Cubs series, Bobby hit two more HR's while Billy only got two hits in the entire series. His only thought was, "this was the last place team, and I still can't get a hit." Once again, he stole a base each time he got on, but in his mind, he had to get his average up if he was going to steal enough bases to be called up by the Royals. He went back to what Mr. Booker told him.....you can't break Ricky's stolen base record if you don't hit around .300. That put even more pressure on him.

Bobby was excited about the next series as it was against his hometown team, the Round Rock Express. They'd won five straight games before coming to Omaha, while the Chasers were fighting to stay above .500. Billy knew that the Royals were hoping each of their minor league teams would win the pennant in their league because that would give them a winning attitude when they reached the majors. So even that put more pressure on Billy because almost as much as being called up this year, he wanted the Storm Chasers to win the AAA title.

The series started well as Tim Morris won the first game on his own, almost. He had a no-hitter until the 8th when the Redbirds got their first hit. By now, the Chasers had scored eight runs, so it was a good feeling for everyone on the team to get the first game win. All except Billy.....he was happy his team had won, but once again, he was hitless. His average was now .167, and he only had six stolen bases the entire season so far. When they got back to the hotel, Billy saw a text from Emma asking him to call her.

He was shocked at his reaction because he didn't even want to talk to her. But, he did as she requested and dialed her number, almost hoping she wouldn't answer.

Her voice sounded good to him, even if he hadn't wanted to call. "Billy, I subscribed to a Major League Baseball app that also showed some minor league games. I've seen you play in four games so far, and in those four games, you only had two hits. I know I'm not a coach, but it was obvious to me what your problem is this year," Emma told him.

"What, Emma?" was all he could say.

"You are over-swinging on just about every pitch," she answered. "It's almost like you are trying to catch Bobby in the HR department. I'm not sure the two of you playing together is helping you."

"No, Emma, I'm not trying to match Bobby," Billy said in a raised voice.

"Do you want to say that in your normal voice, Billy Tankersly?" she fired back at him.

"Emma, you don't know what you are talking about," said Billy, again in a defensive voice.

"OK, don't listen to me, but I suggest you call Mr. Booker because I called him once this season, trying to find out from him what he thought your problem was," Emma said in a calm voice.

"You called Mr. Booker?" Billy asked. "What did he say?".

"Exactly what I told you.....it looks like you are swinging for the fence every time up, and it's putting more and more pressure on you," she responded.

"Mr. Booker said that?" Billy asked.

"Yes, Billy. To those of us who love you, we want nothing more than you to succeed," she said.

Billy had not heard or used that word since telling Bobby that he thought he was in love with Emma.

"Look, Emma, I know you want my best. I do appreciate you calling Mr. Booker," Billy said in a softer voice. He was sort of shocked that he hadn't even thought of Emma the last month as he was so concerned with his own hitting. "Can you drive to Omaha while we are playing the Express, Emma? I'd like to see you."

"After not even getting a call from you in over a month, I don't think it would be best for me to see you right now. I think you need to get your head screwed on properly before I want to spend time with you.....you are acting like a victim now, and that is not the Billy I fell in love with," Emma said, in a straightforward way. Billy was shocked. She was right; he was feeling sorry for himself and not paying attention to anything else.

"Ok, Emma, I will take your advice, and start trying to hit to the opposite field. I've had two managers in my career tell me to hit to the opposite field when in a slump. I've just never been in a slump before, so their words didn't mean that much to me at the time. You are right though, I've been trying to pull the ball every time at bat, and I guess that is what you are seeing when you say I'm trying to kill each pitch," he admitted.

"Good Billy, I'll be looking forward to you hitting at least two balls to left field in the game tomorrow, and I will be watching on my computer," Emma laughed. Billy hadn't heard her laugh in a long time now, and it reminded him why he thought he was in love with her. He didn't tell her, but the reason he hadn't called was not that she was out of his thoughts, but he just didn't want to talk to anyone while in this slump. Who wants to hear someone complain, he thought?

"Emma, I've got to go, but thank you for having me call you, and the good advice you always give," Billy said with a much lighter tone than the way the call started. "I'm sorry I haven't called, and I promise that slump or not, I will keep in touch," he ended the call.

Billy went to sleep that night feeling better than he had in a month. He snuggled with his bat, and his last thought before going to sleep was, "I'm going to get two hits to left field tomorrow."

# 5

## He Takes Emma's Advice

Billy woke, more excited than any time during the last month. He could see himself hitting two singles to left field and stealing two bases.

The game started with Billy now hitting 6th since the manger felt that would take some of the pressure off his potential star. No matter whether it was hitting 6th or the call with Emma, Billy felt relaxed as he came up in the second inning of a scoreless first inning for both teams. He was determined to hit the ball to left on the first hittable pitch. As it turned out, the first pitch was over the plate, and sure enough, he lined a single to left field. The bench all yelled, "Way to go, Billy. Now steal second." He heard them, and it felt good.

On the second pitch to Aaron Troup, the DH for the Storm Chases, Billy got the steal sign and was safe at second by "a country mile," Emma heard the announcers describing the game. She was proud of Billy for keeping to his word and hitting one to left field.

The game rolled on, with the Chasers leading 3-1 when Billy got up again. He waited for a pitch he could hit, and instead of trying to pull it, he hit a line drive to left field for a single. Again, he stole 2nd base, and on the next pitch, stole third base. Wow, that felt good to Billy. Maybe Emma's advice was just what he needed. He scored on a sacrifice fly off the bat of Christian Louis, the Catcher for the Chasers. Now, it was 4-1, and the team never looked back.  They kept scoring runs, and by the time Billy got up again, the score was 7-1.  He was determined to get another hit and steal at least one more base. He waited for a fastball and hit it to left field for his third hit of the game.  Unfortunately, Christian hit into double-play on the first pitch, and Billy didn't get to steal, but he had three hits in a game for the first time all season, and all were to left field.  The game ended with no more runs by either team, and Billy flied out to left his last time up.  He was thrilled, 3 for 4, and three stolen bases.  He even laughed at dinner after the game, telling Bobby that now he had to chase Billy for the most hits in the season, even if Billy would never catch him in the HR department. He felt his confidence coming back.

The Storm Chasers won the next two games as well against the Express.  Bobby hit two HR's in the last two games, and Billy had three hits, all to left field.  He also had three stolen bases and felt like the 'old Billy' had returned.

The team had to catch the bus almost immediately after the game because they were headed to San Antonio to play the Missions and then to Austin to play the Round Rock Express in two "away series" before returning back to Omaha.  The first game against the San Antonio Missions, who were in the Southern Division of the American Conference, was a runaway victory for the Chasers. Billy had two more hits, two steals, and Bobby had a long, long HR.  Emma was watching this game as it was being televised on the Minor League portion of the MLB app.  She laughed when she heard the announcers talking about how far Bobby's HR traveled.  One of the announcers said he'd never seen a ball hit that far, even in the majors. She just wished they'd talk more about Billy's two hits and stolen bases.

After winning two more in San Antonio, the Chasers were now in first place as they traveled up the road about 90 miles to the Express Stadium. Billy remembered playing there on the travel team and thinking it was the most beautiful park he'd ever played in......and he felt the same as they walked into the Stadium. The bus had to drive through Austin, Bobby's hometown, and the only thing he said was, "I can't believe how fast Austin is growing." Billy remembered staying at the Hyatt Regency in Austin when they played there, but this time, it was a little hotel about three miles from the Stadium.
Bobby's Mom and Dad met the bus as the team arrived. Billy thought how good it was to see them again. Bobby hugged them both. As when the travel team came to Austin, Bobby's folks said, "OK, boys, tonight you get a good meal. Both boys laughed and said, "have you been following us into the crummy restaurants the team eats at when on the road?" Bobby's folks laughed, got them into their car, and headed through a part of town Billy had not seen before.

"Billy, I know Bobby likes Indian food, do you?" they asked.

"Heck, I don't know. I've never had Indian food; I don't think," Billy replied.

"Well, we are going to the Clay Pit that I think you will love," Bobby's Mom said.

They drove down a street that was close to the University of Texas. They came upon a building that looked like many of the buildings in New Orleans.

When they went inside, it looked even older than the building in New Orleans, but the aroma of the food had to be the best smell Billy had ever smelled.

Bobby laughed as Billy was taking it all in. Bobby thought, " Kansas City doesn't have any place like this." Billy asked what he should order, and Bobby ordered for Billy. It was, without a doubt, the best dinner he'd ever had. He found out he loved Indian food.

After dinner, Bobby's folks drove them back to their small motel, and it was quite obvious they had missed Bobby. Billy told Bobby to spend a little more time with his folks as Billy went to their room. He thought, maybe he should call Emma.

"Hi, Coach," Billy said as Emma answered the phone. "It appears my coaching has helped, Mr. Tankersly," Emma started, laughing, just happy that Billy had called. "I guess the Royals need to hire you because I followed your advice and came out of my slump the first game I hit the ball to left field," Billy chimed in. "And boy, oh boy, did that feel good, Emma. Thank you so much for your advice."

The two talked until Bobby came up to the room. "Ok, Coach, I've got to go now. I love you," Billy said, surprised that it came out of his mouth so easy. Bobby looked at him and said, "So you are now telling the coaches you love them?" he laughed. "No, Bobby, I was talking to Emma," like Bobby had been serious in his comment as he entered the room. He knew darn well who Billy was talking to, and happy for Billy to be calling her. Once again, without Billy knowing, Bobby had talked to Emma twice during Billy's slump and was aware of why Billy hadn't called her. He told Emma to be patient, and once

Billy got out of his slump, he'd call her. He had a sneaky suspicion that Emma had talked to Billy and advised him to hit to left.

The Storm Chasers added to their three game sweep in San Antonio by sweeping three games. Billy had a smile on his face once again. He remembered a young boy by the dugout in the first game who had a KC cap on, and one inning as Billy came in after catching a popup to end the inning, the young boy said, "Hey Billy, can I have that ball?" that Billy still had in his glove. He smiled at the youngster and said, "sure," as he tossed him the ball. He wondered how many balls this kid had, as he was not shy, but Billy could tell, the kid loved baseball, and he reminded Billy of himself about that age.

After the last game before boarding the bus back to Omaha, Bobby hugged his folks like he'd never hug them again. It was great seeing Bobby so happy. On the bus ride back to Omaha, Billy told Bobby about the youngster, and Bobby replied by saying, "you'd be surprised at how many KC fans live in Austin."

# 6

## West Coast Trip

The remaining schedule to the All-Star game had the Storm Chasers playing teams from the Southern Division of the Pacific Conference and then two teams in the Northern Division of the Pacific Coast Conference. It was a long bus ride to Salt Lake City, where they swept the Bees, and then it was to Las Vegas, which was exciting to both Billy and Bobby since they'd never been to Vegas before. Of course, they were both too young to order drinks, but it was fun on their off day just walking the streets of Vegas. They loved the downtown area, but the most exciting part was going to the top of the Stratosphere Hotel, that was 110 floors high. On the top was a roller coaster that seemed to go off the building at times, which scared both boys, especially when they saw a 737 airplane flying lower than they were. The highlight was a bungee-type ride that went up another 15 floors. Both boys were expecting a slow ride to the top and then a sudden drop. Were they ever surprised when it shot them up at a 4G force to the top, and then they seemed to hang for a long time. The view was beyond belief, 125 floors above the ground until they started falling almost to where they started, and then it slung them up again. When they got off, Bobby was the first to speak.

"Billy, that was the scariest ride I've ever been on. I thought the roller coaster 110 floors up was scary, but nothing like the Big Shot Ride," laughed Bobby to where everyone in Vegas must have heard him. Billy was still catching his breath from the ride and decided he'd never go on that again. Both boys wore themselves out, walking all over Vegas and going on the rides at the top of the Stratosphere. They hit the sack about 9:00 PM, Vegas time, which would have been 11:00 PM back in Omaha. They had to be on the field for batting practice and infield practice by 1:00 the next day.

The three games in Vegas seem to be over before they started. Again, the Chasers swept the second team on their west coast trip to take sole possession of first place. Billy only had two hits and one stolen base the entire series, but once again, Bobby was hitting HR's. He hit a total of four HR's in the series against the Bees and Aviators, which both boys thought was a good name for the Vegas team after they'd seen the passenger jet flying into Vegas lower than they were on top of the Stratosphere.

From Vegas, the team went to Sacramento, where they were playing the River Cats, who always had a good team. This year, the River Cats were 22-10 going into the series, while the Storm Chasers were 24-8, so it was going to be another series, where they had to win to stay in first place.

Tim King was pitching for the Chasers. He was turning into the ace of the team with a 2.43 ERA. By the 4th inning, Tim had only allowed two hits while the Chasers had scored four runs, one a hit and stolen base for Billy. Once again, Bobby hit a HR to score Billy, even though Billy was sure he could steal third on their pitcher. By the time they reached the 9th inning, Billy had another hit and was able to steal 2nd and 3rd, so he was beginning to feel like he was on top of his game again. In the 7th inning, a ball was hit sharply to his right that he backhanded, jumped in the air, and threw the runner out, thanks to Bobby stretching as far as he could to get the ball in his glove before the runner got to 1B. At the end of the inning, the coaches slapped Billy on his butt and told him that was one of the best plays they'd seen all year. That pretty much took the wind out of the River Cats, and now the Chasers were 25-8, while the River Cats lost their 11th game. That meant if the Chasers could sweep the next two games, they were almost assured of being in first place by the All-Star break.

It didn't happen as Billy went silent again without getting any hits, and Bobby had a couple of hits, but no HR's, so the team was still in first place, but by only a couple of games. They left for Tacoma to play the Rainiers, who were in last place. Most on the team felt they could sweep the Rainiers, but once again, the entire team's bats went silent the first game. They were shutout by the last place, Rainiers. It was only the second time all year they had been shut out. The coaches gathered the team by the dugout after the game to give them a pep talk.

"Listen, guys; we've played great ball all year. Since this is our last trip before the All-Star break, let's finish it out by winning the next two," Coach Temple said in a matter of fact way.

The pep talk did good as the team won the next two, but Billy did not have a hit. He was now above the Mendosa line, but just barely hitting .234. After the game, the coach called them all together again.

"Guys, I have great news. Bobby will not be joining us back in Omaha because the Royals are calling him up." Everyone cheered except Billy. He fully expected to get a call up before Bobby, but it was no one's fault but his own.  He knew he had to have a great second half, or he would not be called up at all this year.

"Bobby, that is great," Billy said as he hugged his best friend.  Bobby knew Billy was disappointed, but he wasn't thinking about Billy right now.....he had just learned he was going to the bigs, and it would be his first time of being called up.

"Billy, you've just been putting too much pressure on yourself, or you'd be going up with me," said Bobby, trying to cheer his best friend up.

"Yeah, I know, Bobby," and I am happy for you, even if being disappointed in my own play so far this year," spoke Billy in a softer voice than Bobby ever remembered hearing his best friend speak.  "Hey Bud, you'll be up by the end of the year, and we'll be together again," said Bobby in a forceful way.

"I'd better start hitting, or I'll end up being 19 before getting back to the Royals," said Billy.  Bobby laughed.  "All of 19, eh."  "Billy, after getting a taste of playing with the Royals last year, I really thought I'd be called up by the All-Star break, but the way I've been hitting, I may not even get 25 stolen bases this year," said Billy, with a frown on his face.

The bus ride back to Omaha was the longest he'd ever been on.  He sat next to Mack, who raved about Bobby being called up.

"Mack, Bobby has been my best friend since we were 6 or 7 years old, so I'm extremely happy for him, but disappointed in myself for having such a crappy year so far," Billy moaned.  "In fact, how many stolen bases do you have....I'll bet it's more than me."  Mack laughed, saying, "Billy, I'll never have more stolen bases than you, no matter how badly you are hitting."

When arriving in Omaha, there was a message at the motel desk for Billy to call Emma.  She was the last person he wanted to talk to right now, but he dialed her number.

"Hi, Billy," she answered. "Hey, I know you are disappointed that Bobby beat you up to the Royals this year, but don't get down on yourself.....I want you to come to Lexington over the break."

"Emma, I'd like to do that, but I have to go home to see my folks," replied Billy.  "OK, Billy, would you mind if I come to KC to be with you for a couple of days?" she asked.

"I don't think you should, Emma.  I need to spend time with Dad and Mom and see Mr. Booker while there," answered Billy.

Her heart was broken.

# <u>7</u>

## Billy Ready To Quit

"Mr. Booker, as you know, I'm having a terrible year," started Billy as he saw his old mentor. "I have no idea what I'm doing wrong."

"Well Billy, I've seen a few games on TV, and it looks to me like it's a simple matter.....you are not waiting for your pitch," Mr. Booker said, matter of factly.

"That's it," Billy quizzed Mr. Booker.

"From the games I've seen, you are swinging at pitches not even close to the plate. It's like you are getting fooled on every pitch," Mr. Booker explained more in-depth. "Do you want to go up to the practice field and hit a few?" he asked.

"Sure, Mr. Booker."

So both went to the practice diamond where Billy had learned the most in his 18 years.

"Johnny, can you throw a few to Billy Tankersly?" he asked Johnny Trombone, who was now in charge of the facility.

"You mean the famous Billy Tankersly," Johnny replied.

Billy answered, "Not famous enough to get on base enough to break Ricky's stolen base record."

Mr. Booker told Johnny he wanted him to start with some curves.

Billy got in the cage and swung at the first pitch he saw.

"See, Billy, that wasn't even close to the plate," Mr. Booker said, "That's what I've seen in the games I watched."

"OK, Johnny mix some fastballs with some curves," Billy's mentor instructed Johnny.

One pitch after another, Billy swung, missing almost all of the pitches off the plate.

"OK, Billy, I can see exactly what's wrong with your game," Mr. Booker said.

"Obviously, I'm not seeing the ball," Billy quipped.

"Billy, it's not a matter of you not seeing the ball, it's a matter of you not waiting for your pitch," Mr. Booker told him.

"Mr. Booker, when I first got to the Lexington team last year, the coach told me that the Royals played with the intention of getting on base, even if we swung at bad pitches," explained Billy.

"That is not what you were taught," Mr. Booker corrected him. "You were taught to swing at pitches that were hittable, not pitches way off the plate."

"So you are telling me to wait for my pitch?" Billy asked.

"I'm telling you that if the pitch hits the outside of the plate, swing to get a hit to left field. If it's inside, pull it, but only if it's going to be called a strike if you don't swing." Mr. Booker continued.

"I'm really confused," said Billy. "When I got to Lexington, Coach Keller got on me for letting pitches go by, and he told me, we don't play waiting for our pitch. We play to get on base, and sometimes that means swinging at pitches that are not perfect," Billy explained.

"I think you've carried it a bit more, Billy. The Royals do play to get on base, and with you having the speed you have, the coach was probably trying to get you to recognize when you could hit to left, and when you could pull it."

"Johnny, throw Billy ten pitches on the outside and inside of the plate, either a fastball or a curve," asked Mr. Booker.

Billy stepped back in the batter's box, not knowing what to expect.

The first pitch was outside, and Billy swung.

"Stop Johnny for a minute," the former Major League Grounds Keeper said.

"Billy, that pitch was at least two inches outside. You should have let it go."

"I was trying to hit it to left field," Billy said.

"Well, don't," Billy was even more confused now.

"So what you are saying it, "wait for my pitch and stop trying to hit to left field on the pitches outside," Billy asked.

"Well, if you want to get out of your slump, that would be a wise decision, Billy," his former mentor said in a forceful way.

"OK, Johnny, continue please," Mr. Booker yelled to the pitcher on the mound.

The next pitch was on the outside again, and Billy let it go. Then a curve that broke on the inside of the plate, and Billy let it go by. The next pitch was a fastball over the heart of the plate, and Billy swung, hitting a line drive to centerfield.

"Billy, that was perfect. You didn't try to pull it. You just hit it with the sweet spot of your bat and kept your eye on the ball all the way to bat. I think from what I saw on TV was you turning your head instead of keeping your eye on the pitch from the time it leaves the pitcher's hand," Mr. Booker explained.

Johnny threw seven more pitches. Billy let three of them go by, and Mr. Booker said, "one was a strike, Billy, but the other two were balls. Could you feel the difference?"

"Absolutely, Mr. Booker. The one's I hit reminded me of the way I use to hit," smiled Billy.

"Just remember to keep your eye on the ball from the time it leaves the pitcher's hand until you can see it hit your bat."

Billy remembered that was the feeling he had at Lexington, and again last year when he did spend a little time with the Royals while Skip was injured.

"Thank you, Mr. Booker," Billy said as the two men walked back to the car.

The car stopped in front of the Tankersly home, and for the first time in two months, Billy felt he was going to break out of his slump when the season resumed.

Mrs. Tankersly was at home when Billy returned from working with Mr. Booker. "My dear son, we hardly saw you last night when you got home. I haven't seen you that preoccupied with something since you were in High School worrying about your grades," she commented.

"Mom, I know you've been following me, and I needed to talk to Mr. Booker about my hitting," Billy answered with more pep in his voice since before the break. He knew he had to leave tomorrow for Omaha, so today was going to be spent with his Dad and Mom. "What time does Dad get home?" he asked his Mom. "He's taking half a day off, so he can spend it with you, Billy," his Mom replied. "What time will he be home, Mom?" Billy asked, anxious to see his Dad.

He should be home within 30 minutes, son," answered his Mom.

"Mom, I have a question for you," Billy said.

"What Billy?" Mrs. Tankersly asked.

"Do you think I should keep going with baseball, or quit?" Billy asked.

"What kind of a question is that?" she asked.

"Well, as I'm sure you know, I have not been able to hit anything the past two months. I'm pretty depressed about the entire thing. I worked so hard to get there, but now that I'm at Omaha and can't hit anything here, how in the world am I going to be able to hit in the majors if I ever get back there?" Billy commented and asked at the same time.

"Billy, ask your Dad when he gets home," she replied.

Just then, Billy heard his Dad pull into the driveway. He went running outside to give his Dad a big hug.

When they got inside, it was his Mom who brought up what Billy had asked his Mom.

"What in the world are you talking about, Billy?" his Dad asked with total disbelief that this was his son asking the question.

"Dad, I know you've been following me even if you haven't come up to see me play," Billy was close to having tears in his eyes.

"Billy Tankersly, we would have been up to several games, but we've been watching you and the games they televised, and we just thought it would put more pressure on you," his Dad replied. "It's been obvious, you did not need more pressure, son," his Dad reassured him.

"You mean you've stayed away just because I was having a bad year?" Billy asked.

"Not necessarily, but this is your first full year at AAA, and we know your goal.  Mom and I just felt that it would not help for us to show up when you're mind needs to stay on the game," Mr. Tankersly explained to his son.

"I think that's been half my problem….my mind is only on my game, and as you know, it's sucked," Billy smiled.  "I think I needed this break just to see you," Billy said to his Dad and Mom.

"What time do you have to leave, Billy?" his Dad asked.  "Well, the major league All-Star game is tonight, and I need to leave tomorrow to get back by Thursday," answered the Tankersly's pressured son.

"OK, Billy, let's spend this afternoon out back in our cage.  I'll throw you some pitches like we did before you got drafted," spoke up Billy's Dad.

"That's a deal, let's start now," Billy smiled.

Billy put his old metal spikes on as they walked to the back yard.  "What do you think your problem has been, Billy," asked his Dad.

"Well, I worked out with Mr. Booker yesterday, and he said that I was not waiting for my pitch, but trying to hit every pitch thrown to me."

"That's what it's looked like in the games we've seen on TV," answered his Dad.  "Let me throw you five pitches and see what happens."

Mr. Tankersly threw five pitches, and Billy did not swing at one of them.  "You did that on purpose, Dad, just to see if I would swing at a bad pitch," the 18 year old laughed with his Dad.

"Yep, I did.  On the next five pitches, I'm going to give you two in the strike zone and three outside, or inside," Billy's Dad said.

Sure enough, there were only two good pitches in the next five, and Billy hit them sharply.  And he did lay off the bad ones.

"OK, ten balls this time, and I'm not telling you how many I'll put over the plate," said his Dad.

His Dad knew his son well, and eight of the ten pitches were either curveballs off the plate or fastballs that were close, but Billy felt an ump would have called them balls.  He hit the other two pitched to right field and to left field.

"Good job, Billy.  Eight of the pitches were off the plate, and the two you hit, were strikes, even if not meatballs right down the center," Mr. Tankersly told his son.

This went on for another hour, and Billy's hands were starting to get blisters, or at least it felt that way.  But the main thing was Billy felt confident that he'd done well when the practice was over.

"Dad, thank you for wearing your arm out," Billy laughed.  "I'm ready to quit and feel good about my hitting again.  I will take the lesson of today and start hitting when I get back to Omaha," Billy said.

"Good deal, Billy.  Just keep in mind,  you ARE going to break Ricky's Henderson's stolen base record.  You are only 18, so set your goal for getting back to the Royals by next year....that will give you plenty of time, and keep you from pressuring so much, even if you have a bad game or two," his Dad encouraged him.

Billy hoped someday to be as good a coach as his Dad.

They ate dinner at the kitchen table, just like "old times."  After dinner, they watched the All-Star Game, and Billy saw Skip Anderson starting at SS. He'd followed the Royals as much as he could this year, but had no idea that Skip was having a career year and had made the All-Star team.  More than likely, this meant Skip would sign a long term contract with the Royals that would mean more minor league games for Billy.  He was happy the American League won and was just as glad that Skip didn't get a hit.

The next morning, Billy caught a flight to Omaha.  The Kansas City airport was under major reconstruction, and it took forever for Billy to even get checked in.  His Dad and Mom waved goodbye as Billy was finally getting on the plane.

# <u>8</u>

## Maybe Next Year

Billy was glad to be back in Omaha. He never dreamed he'd think that because playing on the Storm Chasers was not where he wanted to be, but for some reason, he was happy to be there.

It was different not having Bobby at 1B. A Double A player had been promoted to play 1B, and he seemed like a nice kid, maybe a year or two older than Billy. His name was Wally Lopez, and Billy was determined to make him feel at home and not have the pressure that Billy felt the entire first half of the season.

The second half of the season went by fast. Billy was not called up like he'd hoped, but he had regained his confidence at the plate. He ended up hitting .345 the second half and was hoping to be called up to the Royals on the September 1st date, where major league teams were allowed to expand their rosters.

Billy had been following Bobby and knew that he already had 15 HR's and was playing most of the games. The last Billy saw, Bobby was hitting about .280, so Billy figured he was with the Royals to stay. Now, he just had to get called up in the September calls up, so he could at least watch Bobby, knowing that he wouldn't get to play much with Skip still having a career year, even though the Royals were in third place and not close enough to get in the playoffs.

September 1st came, and Billy did not get called up. Mack and Otero both did, but not Billy. The season was over for the Storm Chasers, so all Billy had to do was go back home and then sit in the grandstands watching the Royals the last month of the season.

It was fun watching the Royals play, but even more fun was watching Bobby play. He hit two HR's the first game Billy got to watch. After the game, he met Bobby in the parking lot.

"Holy Smokes, Bobby," said Billy excitedly for his best friend. "I see you haven't lost any of your AAA power," Billy laughed.

"No, Billy, but I was disappointed that you didn't get called up," said Bobby with a frown on his face.

"I think I would have gotten a call-up if Skip wasn't having such a good year, Bobby," said Billy.

"He's had a fantastic year. There's been a lot of talk about him signing a long term contract," said Bobby.

"That's not what I hoped to hear. If Skip signs a long term contract, I hope I get traded to some team where I can play in the bigs, even if it's against you, Bobby," said a discouraged Billy.

The two boys left each other so Billy could get home to talk to his Dad.

"Dad, have you read about Skip getting signed to a long term contract?" Billy asked his Dad over dinner.

"Yes, Billy. There is nothing definite, and he is 37 years old, so I honestly can not imagine the Royals signing him to a long term contract, Billy. But my guess is that they will sign him to a one year contract, or at least they will try to sign him. Other clubs might be interested in Skip, but none will sign him to anything more than a one year deal because of his age.

For the month of September, Billy attended every Royals home game from the grandstands, watching Skip like a hawk. He still had good range on ground balls, both to his right and left, and he continued his good hitting. When Billy got there to watch games, Skip was hitting .295 with 20 doubles and ten HR's. He thought to himself, "that's pretty good for an old man." He was hoping for Skip to go in a prolonged slump like Billy had been in, but that meant the Royals losing. He realized how selfish that was, but he couldn't help it.

During the fifth game that Billy watched from the grandstands, Skip made an error on a fairly easy ground ball. Billy knew he would have not made that error. But, the next inning, Skip hit his 21st double down the right field line. He then scored on a single by Bobby. Billy was excited for Bobby but just couldn't muster up a lot of joy for Skip scoring the winning run.

The Royals played their last home game on September 20th, and all the rest of their games were on the road. Billy got to watch each game on TV with his Dad, and they talked about plays that Skip made or should have made. They also got to watch Bobby continue to hit homers. He finished the season with 20 dingers and had a .286 BA. That meant for sure that Bobby had earned his spot as the regular 1B for the next year and probably years to come. Skip's BA fell to .302, which was still a good year for the Royals SS, and it was almost a certain bet that Skip would be back next year at a minimum.

During the off season, Bobby was offered a three-year contract worth more than Billy had signed for. He was happy for Bobby but kept wondering what the Royals were going to do with Skip. There was a lot of talk about Skip being re-signed as he was a KC favorite, but by January 1st, he still had not been signed. There were rumors that the Houston Astro's were interested in Skip. Then the news broke, Skip had been traded to the Detroit Tigers, and he signed a two-year contract with them. The sports announcers in KC were talking about what the Royals were going to do. Would they bring up that SS from Omaha that only hit .272 last year?

Billy knew his average had been good the second half, but overall, his .272 BA was not quite good enough to get the Royals excited. One announcer said during a 6:00 PM newscast that the Royals were looking to George Pickle, the SS for the Twins last year, hoping to make a trade for him. The rumors made every newscast during January, but by the time Spring Training was starting, no trades had been announced. That meant Billy might be the leading candidate to play SS for the Royals. At least, that's what he hoped, as he waved goodbye to Mr. Booker and his Dad and Mom, who took him to the airport. The flight had to go to Houston before heading to Phoenix. Billy was glad the flight had to go to Houston because he sat next to Bobby on the way to Surprise, Arizona. "Billy, I have a question for you that has been bugging me all winter," Bobby said as the plane took off from KCI.

"Why did the Royals not have you play in the Arizona Fall League like last year?" Bobby asked.

"I don't have a clue, Bobby.  Maybe they felt that since they expected Skip back this year, there was no reason for me to play anymore last year," said Billy, but with a question mark in his voice.

"I've got a different opinion, Billy.  I think they knew they were not going to sign Skip this year, and had you pegged to play the entire year with the Royals," said Bobby.

"Then why didn't they call me up for the September call ups?" Billy asked.

"I have no idea, Billy.  I thought for sure after your great second half, they would call you up.  I mean, you are still on the 40 man roster, so what did they have to lose?" Bobby said outloud as he was trying to figure out why the Royals had not called Billy up last year when the rosters expanded.

"To be honest, Bobby, it upset me a lot`," Billy said, thinking if they knew they would probably trade Skip, why hadn't they called him up.

"I don't think they felt they could get a good trade for Skip and expected him to be here still, is all I can think of, "said Bobby.

"Well, Skip isn't going to be here, so it's my opportunity no matter what," spoke Billy, more to himself than Bobby.

The plane landed in Phoenix, and there was the bus to take them to Surprise.  Spring Training was about to start, and Billy thought back to what Mr. Booker and his Dad had said, "wait for your pitch.'

# <u>9</u>

## Finally!

Billy was excited to see Mack and Arturo and all the other players he'd played with over the past two years, including the major leaguers.

One of the new coaches for the Royals, Tim Sack, was the hitting coach, and he was one of the first coaches to talk to Billy.

"Billy, although it may not seem like it, the Royals followed you closely the past year. We know you were in a slump most of the first half, but after the break, you came back with a great second half. As you know, we did not sign Skip, and that leaves the position wide-open for you," the coach told Billy.

Billy wondered how much this new hitting coach knew. Did the Royals follow him closely last year? How did this new coach know that? As he sat at the space they had for his locker, which was an open locker space instead of one where you closed the door to your locker, Billy wondered if the Royals followed him closely. He knew one thing. With Skip gone, there was no reason why he should not be starting at SS. He just had to prove it to them in Spring Training.

Another major change with the Royals was George Kessler being promoted to the manager position. Coach Kessler had been the manager at Omaha, so if he ever had a chance to start the season as SS, this might be the best chance he'd ever have. Billy figured the hitting coach Tim Sack knew about him because of Coach Kessler. All the signs were there that Billy was going to be given the chance to start at SS this year.

The first day of Spring Training started with a lot of running and starting to get in shape. What the Royals didn't know was that Billy had worked all winter in getting in shape and adding muscle, which increased his weight to 205 pounds. He ran the outfield with everyone, and let others take the lead in finishing first. He had no intention of "showing off" his speed the first day of Spring Training. It was at this point; Billy realized he had his confidence back. It excited him to think that he might start at SS and then have a spectacular year. After running the outfield, Bobby came over to him.

"Hey Mr. SS, are you going to challenge me in HR's this year," Bobby kidded him. It didn't hit Billy at the time, but even Bobby's words seem to indicate everyone in the organization knew Billy was slated to be the starting SS for the Royals this year.

Sure enough, in the Royals first Spring Training game, being played at Surprise, Billy was starting at SS and hitting 8th. His first time up, he walked, stole second, and scored on a double by Bobby. In the 4th inning, Billy finally got up again, as it had been a pitcher's duel in the first part of the game.

Billy led off in the 4th inning and promptly hit a line drive between left field and center field, and easily turned it into a double with his speed. Bobby struck out, so with one out, Billy was surprised to see the third base coach give him the steal sign. They must have seen something about the pitcher that made them think Billy could steal third base in his first game.

Billy took a slightly bigger lead than he normally would, forgetting he was in the majors, and pitchers could tell if a baserunner had even a one-foot advantage. The pickup throw to second was a warning to Billy to stay right where he was, as Billy had to dive to reach the base before the tag.

On the pitch, Billy took off for third base. "Safe," yelled the ump. The next batter, Tim Owens, the centerfielder, who had been traded to the Royals for Jim Swift, a pitcher for Omaha last year, hit a short fly ball to center. Billy timed it perfectly and scored the first run on Swift's sacrifice fly ball. The team ignored him when he reached the dugout. He couldn't figure it out. Weren't all the players on the same team and scoring a run in what had been a shutout against the Royals. Billy expected them all to give him high-fives as he reached the dugout.

After about 30 seconds, they all starting cheering Billy. They pounded him on the back, on the head, and gave him high-fives. Every member of the team made a point to congratulate Billy. He felt like he was finally a KC Royals player.

Billy had one more hit in the game and again stole second, even when the other team was now expecting it. This time, Bobby came through with a massive HR over the left-field fence, giving the Royals a three-run lead which they never relinquished. Billy's first game in Spring Training was an indication of just how fast he was, and now with more muscle and weight, he was hitting the ball with authority. The rest of Spring Training was a confidence builder for Billy as he finished Spring Training with a .385 BA and had 12 stolen bases. The other teams just could not throw him out.

When the regular season started, Billy was in awe. He was finally a Kansas City Royals. He was at SS, batting fifth, right behind Bobby. The two boys had spent most of Spring Training with each other after the games, and Bobby could not have been more encouraging to Billly. Afterall both boys thought Billy would be called up before Bobby, but the baseball gods had a different idea. Bobby had fit in with the team nicely last year, and the Royals signed him to a five-year contract during the winter, which was on top of the earlier contract he'd signed. Billy hoped he could make the same impression as Bobby had.

The game started with Goose Tyson, who had been promoted last year, being named as the starting pitcher for Minnesota. The game was being played in Minneapolis, and it was cold. Billy had long wondered why the major leagues seemed to always have one or two teams playing in stadiums up north, starting the season.

Just like in Spring Training, Billy started hot. He led off the second inning after Bobby flied out for the third out in the first inning. He waited for his pitch and hit one into the right field corner. He saw the right fielder bobbled the ball for just a second and knew he could reach third base for a triple. It was a close call at 3rd base, but Billy was safe with his first triple. Pete Lorenze, who was a definite pull hitter, saw "the switch," which had become part of baseball in the last few years. With all the information available, the coaches had proof on their computers about where a player would hit the ball. Pete saw that the 3rd baseman was playing almost to 2nd base, leaving all of the third-base line open for a hit that direction.   Billy watched Pete all last year and was ready for what was about to happen.  He laid down a bunt toward third base, and not only did it score Billy, Pete was safe at first base.

Billy wondered how long it would take other teams to realize that Pete was an intelligent player who would take advantage of every opportunity presented to him.

The Royals won the game with Billy getting two more hits, both singles, which allowed him to steal. And steal he did.  Two more stolen bases and Billy felt he was on his way to breaking Henderson's stolen base record.  Add the three steals to what he did last year when being called up with Skip on the DL, and he now had seven stolen bases...a long way to go to break Ricky's record, but Billy was only 19, starting for the Royals, whereas Ricky had been 20 when he started his streak.  Billy felt he was already ahead of Ricky and was thrilled.

After the game, Billy and Bobby went to a famous steakhouse in Minneapolis, Murry's steak house.  They both ordered a filet that had to be one of the best steaks either boy had experienced.  Billy was really surprised as he thought the steak houses in KC were supposed to be the best in America.  But, as the boys talked while eating, Billy was impressed with Murry's.

Billy spoke sort of softly, "Bobby, I could care less about this steak house; I'm more excited about the game today, and the rest of the season to come."

The two best friends left Murry's with one thing on their mind, "winning a pennant for the Royals.

# <u>10</u>

## Side Trip To Lexington

Before they knew it, it was time for the All-Star game. Neither Billy nor Bobby were selected to represent the American League, but that did not matter to either of them. The Royals were in first place by three games, and both boys had contributed greatly. Bobby, although not leading the league in HR's, was third with 18 HR's. Billy was having a fantastic year in the field, making one highlight film after another. But, he was most proud of his hitting and stolen base record so far. He was hitting .298 and had 36 stolen bases to lead the league.

On the flight back home, he wasn't able to find how many stolen bases Ricky had by the All-Star break, but Billy found out that he only played in 84 games his first year and stole 33 bases. He had been thrown out 11 times. It was the second year when Ricky Henderson started his long streak of leading all of baseball in steals. 100 steals in 158 games and 591 At Bats in his first full year.

None of the Royals were on this particular flight back to KC, but people several rows back probably heard Billy say, "Holy Mackeral," when he saw what Ricky did his first full year.

When he arrived at the KC airport, his Dad and Mom were waiting for him, and after giving them both hugs, Billy said, "Let's get out of here, I'm tired of airports." They both laughed, knowing the travel schedule of a big leaguer was hectic, although not as bad as the rickety bus Billy had described at Lexington his first year.

After dinner, Billy said he was exhausted and looked forward to sleeping on his own bed. He kissed his Mom goodnight and gave his Dad a big hug.

As he laid down, all he could think about was Ricky having 100 steals his first full season in the majors. Billy had 33 now and was determined to pick it up the second half. He fell asleep thinking he was going to hit .300 by the end of the year and steal at least 100 bases, as he clutched his sleeping buddy, his bat.

The next morning, his Dad suggested they play catch in the back yard. It was a Sunday morning, and Billy asked his Dad, "aren't you and Mom going to church today?"

"Son, we go almost every Sunday. God, the Bible, and church mean so much to your Mom and me. I know we both felt you'd start going when you got ready, and we didn't want to force you. We've talked about it but still felt you'd join us when you were ready," said Mr. Tankersly as he threw the ball to his son, who was now a major leaguer.

"I remember when we were in Emporia for a travel squad weekend game when I got hurt, and you took me to the hospital," said Billy as he tossed the ball back to his Dad. "I remember praying to be healed, and the next day, the doctor said the injury wasn't as bad as he first feared." That might have been the closest to wanting to go to church, but since that night, I've read the Bible every single night," Billy told his Dad.

"You have?" his Dad asked, taken total off guard. He'd never heard Billy talk about Jesus or God or the Bible, and certainly, not the church.

"I remember that night in Emporia well," said Billy. "You told me to pray, and it would all work out. I had no idea how to pray, but as I laid in that hospital bed, I talked to God and asked him to please let my injury not be as bad as the Doctor indicated. I don't think there has been a night since then, Dad, that I haven't prayed, for you and Mom, and just giving thanks for that day. Of course, in my slump last year, I was having a hard time believing he heard me," laughed Billy.

"You never mentioned it to us, Billy," said his Dad. "Mom and I have not missed a single night of praying together since you were born. Most nights, we pray for you....well, I don't think we've missed a night of praying for you....but we've found that praying together has kept our marriage intact for all these years. When I'm praying each night, I thank God for giving me your Mother," continued Mr. Tankersly, talking about something he did not expect to be talking about.

"I've got a suggestion for you, Billy," his Dad seemed more cheerful than Billy remembered. "Read Mark 11:22-26 when you get a chance...and don't stop with verse 25 like I did for months....read verse 26 as it brings it all together," finished Mr. Tankersly throwing the ball back to Billy.

Billy thought, "I've got to remember that....Mark 11:22-26, Mark 11:22-26 as he repeated it in his mind several times. Mr. Tankersly didn't go through it verse by verse with Billy. He figured he needed to let his son figure it out on his own. The two played catch for a good hour, just talking about Billy's life as a major leaguer. His Dad asked about Emma, and Billy was shocked; it was the first time he'd even thought of Emma this entire season.

"Dad, I think I would make a terrible husband. I haven't even thought of Emma since the start of the season. I've been so wrapped up in playing good ball that .....gezzzz, I have no excuse for not calling her," Billy spurted.

"Well, son, I wouldn't be too worried about it; you are only 19 years old," said Mr. Tankersly to his son. Then again, Billy's Dad did not know Billy had told Emma he was in love with her. Billy felt awful and wondered if she'd talked to Bobby during the season. He hoped she had, but either way, he needed to call her.

After lunch, Billy went into his room and dialed Emma's number. She answered like they'd talked yesterday. "Hi Billy, are you home with your folks over the All-Star break?" she asked.

"Emma, I feel terrible about not calling since our first game," started Billy, somewhat ashamed and embarrassed at the same time.

"Billy, I know you better than you think I do," Emma started. "I've watched almost every game, cheering for you and looking forward to when we did talk. I knew you'd call."

That eased a little of the pressure that Billy felt as he had dialed her number.

"I wish we could watch the All-Star game together," Billy finally said, trying to make up for his lack of attention over the past three months.

"You gonna come to Lexington to see me, Mr. Major Leaguer?" Emma asked, knowing Billy's answer would be 'no'".

"I wish I could, Emma, but I need to spend time with my folks," Billy answered.

"I understand Billy, but I'd like to see you," Emma sorta begged.

"Emma, I wish Lexington was close to any major league stadium so we could meet, but there are not any major league teams near Lexington," Billy said, knowing that Emma wouldn't stay his "girlfriend" if he never saw her. He did miss her even if his mind had been solely on baseball.

Billy started figuring the days before he had to report back to the Royals. Tonight was Sunday night with the HR hitting contest tomorrow night, and then the All-Star game Tuesday night with a travel day for all the teams on Wednesday. He was trying to figure out any time during the next three days where he could fly to Lexington to at least see Emma for a day, but he wanted to watch the All-Star game with his folks.

"What if I catch a red-eye flight after the All-Star game where we could spend all of Tuesday night together?" Billy asked, still trying to figure out if that would work. Since the Royals had their first game after the breakin St. Louis in an interleague game, that would be flying to Lexington one night, and then to St. Louis the next evening, where he could check into the hotel to get some sleep before their game on Thursday.

"Billy, that would be wonderful. Can you do it?" she asked.

"I'm not sure. Let me check the airlines, and I'll call you right back," Billy told his "maybe" girlfriend. It had been six months almost since they'd seen each other, and Billy wondered if she'd changed.

He checked the flight schedules with Southwest Airlines, and there was a flight leaving KC at midnight on the nose. It was a red-eye flight. It only took an hour and a half to fly between the two cities, but still, that would put him into Lexington at 1:30 in the morning.

He went out to the living room and talked to his Dad about it, explaining he had not seen Emma since the start of the season.

"Son, it seems to me that would leave you tired for your opening game with the Cardinals," his Dad replied. "I understand you'd like to see Emma because I know she has followed your career as closely as Mom and I have," Mr. Tankersly told his son. "Something we haven't mentioned to you is that Emma has called us several times, just to say hi to us. She told us she hadn't heard from you and wondered if we'd talked to you," his Dad explained to Billy.

"Maybe this is a better idea. Why not fly to Lexington Tuesday, spend time with Emma on Tuesday afternoon, and then watch the All-Star game with Emma? That would not make it such a rush, rush trip, and you'd get to spend some quality time with Emma," Billy's Dad suggested.

"But I wanted to watch the game with you and Mom," Billy interjected. "I don't even know if Emma is still my girlfriend, Dad. It's been so long since even talking to her, I have no idea where she is at in our relationship, and to be honest, I don't know where

I'm at in any relationship right now," Billy chimed in.

His Dad added, "Well, son, you can do what you think best, but keep in mind that Emma has called us twice just checking in to see if you were OK, so I don't think her feelings about you have changed in the slightest. I can't imagine any girl marrying or even getting serious about a major league ballplayer....that would not be the easiest thing to do because six months...I guess seven....months out of the year, you'd be traveling."

"Dad, if Emma is still interested in me after not calling her all this time, maybe I should go over to see if there is still a spark in our relationship, if you can even call it that," Billy pondered what he would do.

He took another five minutes just sitting in his room, stroking his bat, trying to figure out what he wanted to do. He'd never told anyone, but his bat and metal spikes were his best friend, and he could not imagine anyone getting in the way of him breaking Ricky's record.

"OK, Dad, I'm going to book a flight Tuesday morning," Billy came back into the living room to tell him. His Mom was there, and his Dad had told her about Billy's predicament. His Mom responded, "Billy, I think that is a wise decision because there will be many All-Star games in your career, and this may be the last one you'll be watching on a TV set. Dad and I will watch it together, imagining next year, you being in the starting lineup."

Billy booked the flight and then called Emma back. It had not been "right back" as he'd told Emma, but now he felt at peace doing it this way.

"Emma, I'll be arriving in Lexington at 11:00 AM Tuesday.  We will have that afternoon just to sit and talk about what all has happened in the past six months, and then be able to watch the All-Star game together Tuesday night," Billy explained to her.

"Oh, Billy, that will be wonderful.  I can't tell you how much I've missed you," Emma almost cried on the phone.  That sort of shocked Billy.

# 11

## More Advice From Mr. Booker

Billy spent much of Monday with Mr. Booker, digging for anything else he could tell Billy on how to improve his game.

"Billy, I don't have any great secrets that I haven't discussed with you, Mr. Booker said. "Ahhh, wait a minute. I do have one thing to mention," the Hall of Famer added.

"How many times have you been picked off?" Mr. Booker asked. Billy remembered Mr. Booker had asked him the same question last year.

"One," replied Billy.

"There are advantages to watching a game on TV, as they show how far off the base the runner is. Sam Brown gets off between 11-12 feet. He's not as fast as you, but pitchers worry about him every time he gets on because of the big lead. And not once all year has he been picked off," Mr. Booker added. "All year, I haven't seen you get off more than 10 feet."

"Are you saying I should take a bigger lead, Mr. Booker?" Billy asked

"If you want to break Ricky's record, I'd suggest getting any advantage you can find," said Billy's friend and mentor. "And you might get picked off once or twice, but you shouldn't worry about that, Mr. Speedster. Do you know how many times Ricky got picked off?"

"No," Billy answered.

Mr. Booker laughed. "Neither do I, Billy, but I know some of Ricky's secrets in breaking Lou Brock's record of 938 stolen bases since I was there when Ricky broke the record."

"Are you kidding me? You saw Ricky break the record?" Billy asked in amazement.

"Well, I saw him break Lou Brock's record, not his 1406th stolen base record."

"What secrets are you talking about, Mr. Booker?" Billy asked, wanting to hear more and more.

"Ricky had dinner with Lou after Brock had set the single-season record of 118 steals when he was 35 years old.   Lou told Ricky that he needed to set a goal of breaking that record while he was still young," Mr. Booker explained.

"After that dinner meeting with Brock, Ricky set a goal of having one stolen base every game," Mr. Booker continued.   "The secret to Ricky's success......he set goals each game of how many stolen bases he still needed to break Brock's 118 game steal record in one year, that most players and fans thought would never be broken."

"So how long did it take him to reach that goal?" Billy asked.

"Four years, Billy," answered the best mentor Billy could ever imagine having. "In his 4th year in the majors, at age 24, he stole 130 bases. And every game, he would try to steal as many bases as he could. One game, he got thrown out three times," Mr. Booker laughed.

"He would always take a lead of 3 ½ big steps, which would be about 11-12 feet," he continued. He caused so much havoc that the opposing pitcher walked the next batter many times.

"Ricky was not the most popular player in the game.   He was one of the most disliked players because he was more than confident; he was cocky. He'd talk to the catcher each time up, telling him if he got on base, he was going to steal on the catcher three times in the game," again, Mr. Booker was laughing, remembering Ricky. "When he hit a home run, he'd do a special bat flip, and keep in mind, Billy, Ricky also holds the home run record for leadoff batters."

"I didn't realize that, Mr. Booker," confessed Billy.

"He was an all-around player who was as respected for his power as well as his defensive abilities," added the Hall of Fame Groundskeeper.

Billy was thoroughly enjoying all the information he could get about Ricky Henderson. He had no idea Ricky broke all sorts of records, not just his stolen base record. It was time for Billy to get home to spend a little time with his folks before leaving to see Emma. He hadn't told Mr. Booker yet about his trip to Lexington.

"Mr. Booker, I'm going to fly to Lexington tomorrow to see Emma, so I've got to get home and spend a little time with my parents," Billy said.

As he left, he turned, walked back to Mr. Booker, gave him a big hug, thanking him for all his wisdom that he had given Billy. He didn't notice, but there was a little tear in Mr. Booker's eye. He loved Billy like a son.

That night, Billy watched the HR hitting contest that is always held the night before the All-Star game with his Dad and Mom. They kept making bets on who would hit the most. It was a night Billy would cherish, but by the end of the evening, he was thinking about Emma.

He packed, told his Dad and Mom that the Royals returned home in the third series after the break, and he would spend more time with them then.

He caught the 10 AM flight, and the plane touched down in Lexington at exactly 11:30 AM. As Billy walked down the ramp to get off the plane, he saw Emma. She was gorgeous.

<h1 style="text-align:center"><u>12</u></h1>

## Emma Going To KU

"Emma, you look so beautiful," Billy said in a higher than normal voice.

"Billy, it is so good to see you," Emma replied, ignoring his "beautiful" remark.

"What do you have planned for the day?" Billy asked.

"I considered going to the Lexington museum," Emma smiled.

"You are kidding, right?" asked Billy, wondering what in the world why he'd want to see the Lexington museum. He didn't even know there was a museum in Lexington.

Emma tried her best to keep a straight face but burst out laughing. "Billy, I don't even know if we've got a museum here," she laughed again.

"How about if we just go to the park and have a picnic?" she asked as she threw her arms around Billy, giving him the sweetest hug he'd ever felt.

"You know what, Emma, I don't care what we do as long as you are by my side," Billy said as he squeezed her tighter.

They walked to Emma's car and headed toward Lexington Park, right by the river.

"I've got some news to tell you anyway," said Emma as she pulled out a blanket and a picnic lunch.

"What is the news, Emma?" Billy asked.

"Well, while you were playing baseball, I've been studying, really hard to get a scholarship offer.  I want to major in sports management," Emma started to let Billy know a little more about her plans.

"I followed your example, Billy. I set a goal and then worked harder than anyone else in my class to reach it. I had several full scholarship offers in sports management.  In reality, I knew after one visit; I wanted to be a KU Jayhawk," she exclaimed excitedly.

Billy was silent for a good 30 seconds before replying. "Are you  kidding me?"

"I thought you'd be excited, Billy, but obviously you're not," sputtered Emma.

Again, Billy was silent for a few seconds, collecting his thoughts.

Emma spoke again.  "Billy, you told me you loved me, and I figured by going to KU, we could be together more.  You thanked me for being your coach last year, and I figured I could help you keep your mind on breaking Ricky's record," she confided her thoughts to him.

"Emma, you may be right.  But what if I start thinking about you instead of baseball?" he asked. "It would be easy as when we are together, I forget about everything else," continued Billy, trying to wrap his mind around her being at KU.

"Well, that is the last thing I'd want, Billy.  I have dated other boys while you were playing, but all I could think of was you," Emma confessed.

"Have you accepted the offer?" Billy wanted to know just how serious she was.

"Yes," Emma replied.

"Em," he never called her that. "I'm not sure what I think," Billy admitted.  "When we've been together, not once have you ever put anything else over my goal of breaking Ricky's record. You've always encouraged me; you've even pointed out things that would help," he admitted to her, and himself as well. He was getting excited at the thought of them being close to each other.

He took her in his arms in front of everyone at the park.

"It took a minute for me to grasp the fact that we could be together. I think this is fantastic news," Billy said as he hugged her even tighter and kissed her on the lips.

"Billy, you didn't seem so sure at first," she had tears in her eyes.

"Em, I think this is great news. I have missed you, but my mind is so focused on breaking Ricky's record that my first thought was, will I be distracted?" he confessed to her.

"Billy, I will never do anything to distract you. When we are together, I promise only to encourage you. I want you to break Ricky's recond almost as much as you do," Emma said.

"You know," continued Emma. "My thoughts were more along the lines of would you distract me from attaining my goal?"

Billy laughed, finally at ease with Emma moving to Lawrence, KS., only minutes on K-10 from his house. He figured she would go to summer school, so she really wouldn't be around him during the season.

"What are your overall plans, Em?" he asked, hoping she would not say she was going to summer school as well.

"Well, Billy, I truly believe that I can get into sports management with a baseball team, because I am good at it, as my grades showed. If I go to summer school, I'll be able to start doing what I want to do, just like you want to break Ricky's recond," she told him.

Again, Billy didn't say anything for a few seconds as he mulled it all around in his mind.

"First off, Em," he started pouring out his thoughts. "I have been thinking about this very selfishly since you told me." I hadn't even thought; I might get in your way of achieving your goals."

"You have helped me in my career so far, even if I haven't kept in touch. The last thing in the world I'd want would be to get in your way of accomplishing your goals," Billy admitted to Emma. I will only encourage you, as you have me," Billy said excitedly.

"Rock Chalk Jayhawk," Billy laughed. "This will be great, Em."

I'm excited for you and will do all I can to help you," Billy exclaimed.

"The two of them were meant for each other," Billy thought.

# 13

## Interesting Day Off

They held hands as they walked through Lexington. Billy wanted to see the ballpark where his career started, so they took an Uber to the newly named Whitter Bank Ballpark. When Billy played there, it was the Applebee's Ballpark. There were no games being played as it was the All-Star break, so Billy talked his way past the security guard telling him he played his first professional game there and was now a Kansas City Royals.

Billy and Emma walked down to the field. Billy led Emma toward home plate. He stood there, looking around and remembering his first game. He remembered thinking, this is a memory I'll never forget.

"Em, this is great, remembering my first game here. I'm sure you weren't at the game when I first arrived," said Billy.

"You'd be surprised, Billy. I was at that game, and I remember this new player that just arrived, standing at home plate, looking around before he stepped into the batter's box," Emma told Billy. "I remember thinking, that looks like a nice boy. I hope he stays at our house while in Lexington."

"No way, Emma," laughed Billy. "I suppose you even suggested to your folks to let me live with you while in Lexington."

"Yes, sir. I did," admitted Emma. "You were able to stay with us because I told my folks about this nice looking boy and asked them if he could stay with us. They agreed.”

“Wow, Em, was this love at first sight for you, as I fell in love with the ballpark?” laughed Billy.

“I guess it was,” laughed Emma. Both were laughing, and Billy felt almost as good as stealing his first base.

The two left the park and went back to Emma's house to watch the All-Star game. Her folks were just as glad to see Billy as he was in seeing Emma. The game was a good one with the American League winning in the bottom of the 9th.` Jon Foster, a starting pitcher for the Royals, was the only Royals selected for the game, and he got to pitch one inning in relief. Billy was glad for him that he shut the National League down in order.

Emma's Mom asked Billy if he'd like to spend the night in his old room? Even though he had already paid for the motel, he gladly accepted. Billy and Emma sat on the front porch for an hour or so just like when he was with the Legends. When he went to his room, he laid there for 30 minutes, thinking back to his days in Lexington. It was good to be back.....and especially seeing Emma.

The next morning, Emma asked him if he'd like to see the University of Kentucky. Billy had told her they were rivals for having the best team in college basketball, not just this year, but in the history of college basketball. He then asked her how much she knew about college basketball.

“Billy, I live in Lexington,” she replied sarcastically like that was the only town for college basketball.

"Do you know who James Naismith is?" Billy asked.

"No, who is that?" she quizzed him.

"He is the founder of basketball and was the first coach at KU. He was the only losing coach KU has ever had," said Billy. "When he invented the game, using peach baskets for the baskets at each end of the court, dribbling was not allowed. The original rules are in a museum at Allen Field House," Billy said proudly like he was a KU Jayhawk.

"Do you know who Adolph Rupp is?" Billy asked.

"No," she smiled.

"Well, he played for KU and then began coaching at Kentucky," Billy started. "He played for Phog Allen, the second KU coach, and then went on to become the best coach in America, right behind Phog Allen," Billy laughed.

As they walked around the University of Kentucky, Billy thought, Emma is going to love KU compared to this. He smiled as he told her that. She smiled back, saying, "Billy, I've already been to KU. I had to go there on a visit to make sure I was going to accept the scholarship, from KU." Then she laughed, as did Billy. Guess he wasn't going to be able to sell her on KU....it was more like she was selling him on the school.

He had to catch his flight to St. Louis, where the Royals opened their second half of the season. The Cardinals were in first place in the National League, and the Royals were in first place in the American League. As they drove to the airport, Emma sat close to Billy and thanked him over and over for flying to Lexington. As he got out and unloaded his suitcase, Emma came around to kiss him. He liked it, and all the way to St. Louis on the Southwest Airlines flight, it was that kiss that kept popping into his mind. Finally, he broke away from Lexington and Emma and got his mind back on breaking Ricky Henderson's record. After what he'd learned from Mr. Booker earlier, he was determined to steal a base for each game they played, just like Ricky had done.

# <u>14</u>

## Billy Gets Hot

The Cardinal series lived up to its billing.  The Royals lost the first game 6-5, but Billy got two hits and two stolen bases, even though he didn't score at all.  The second game was just as thrilling.  The Royals won the game, 3-2.  Billy was the hero for the Royals with two hits and again, two stolen bases, but this time he scored both times.  Before the third game, Coach Kessler got the team together and brought up the fact that these two teams could end up in the World Series. He encouraged the team to play their best tonight to put the Cardinals on notice that if they did play each other in the World Series, they should be a little worried.  The Coach laughed and said, "I think I just predicted our first pennant in many years."

Again, Billy had two hits for the third consecutive game and keeping to his goal; he had two stolen bases.  They could not catch him.  He was taking a little bigger lead as Mr. Booker had suggested.  Billy was shocked at how much of a difference it made.  Not once in the entire series had they even come close to getting Billy, and they knew he was going to steal.  In the third game, they called a pitchout, and Billy still beat the throw.  It was his third straight game of getting two hits and stealing two bases.  It put his batting average over .300, and he now had 39 stolen bases.  He realized that on the surface, there was no way he'd get 100 stolen bases like Ricky did his first full season, but setting a goal of one stolen base per game meant that he would end up with 88 stolen bases. He thought, "why not two stolen bases a game like this past series?" That would put him ahead of Ricky's record. Of course, he'd have to get on base at least two times each game. He laughed at that because he'd end up with a batting average of more than .350 for the season. Some things are possible, so he thought, just keep doing what he did in this series. The Royals won the third game, 8-4, and headed to Cincinnati to play the Reds. Cincinnati had a losing record at the break for the first time in four years but had won three straight against Atlanta.

Tom King started the first game for the Royals and pitched six innings of no-hit ball, but in the 7th, they nailed him for two runs before Terry Wisner came in to relieve him. Wisner was a lefty and had the Reds swinging at pitches two inches off the plate. His curve to left-handed batters made the hitter think he was going to be hit with the ball before it broke to the outside of the plate. The game was tied, 2-2 when Wisner came in, and normally he would only pitch one inning before bringing in Dusty Jenkins and then Nomar Gomez. Ho was the closer. But tonight, Coach Kessler let Wisner pitch the 8th since he only threw seven pitches in the 7th. Billy led off the 8th and hit his 14th HR to put the Royals up by one. Then Bobby drove one into the left-field bleachers for back to back homers to give the Royals a two-run lead. Nomar closed out the game, and the Royals now had a five game lead in the Central Division with the White Sox losing two games at Detroit. Billy's HR was good, but it was his only hit, so no stolen base this game. He did remember Ricky led the majors in HR's, hitting from the leadoff spot.  So he was glad he was starting to show some power as well as his speed.

After the game, Billy had dinner at a restaurant close to the hotel where the team was staying.  It was a Hyatt Regency and reminded Billy of his first trip to Austin.  Bobby sat next to Mack, who also had a good year for the Royals after making the team in Spring Training.  The two of them, having played together at Lexington and then Omaha were the hottest double-play combination in the majors.  It made no difference which player started it, the other touched second base, and at almost the exact same time as touching the base, the ball was on its way to first.  Both players had strong arms, so their double plays were almost as fun to watch as their hitting.

"Billy," Mack started. "I have a question for you. What is the change in your base-stealing since the first half....you've been hot, to say the least," added Mack.

"It's funny you asked because I was just thinking about that.  When I was at home over the break, I spent time with my former mentor ....well, I guess he's still my mentor. He asked how many times I'd been picked off, and then explained what Ricky Henderson did in his game.

"What did Ricky do?" Mack asked.

"Well, he always took 3 ½ steps from first base, which was about 11-12 feet off the base," Billy answered.  "But he wasn't afraid of being picked off. In fact, in one game, he got picked off three times. That made me not worry about getting picked off by getting a foot more off the base than I was doing the first half.  So I started taking that extra foot.....and found out, I could still dive back to first on a pickoff.

You've seen the difference obviously since you asked what I'd changed.....and that's it," Billy finished.

"Oh, one other thing, Mr. Booker told me that Ricky did. He set goals each day of how many bases he was going to steal," added Billy.

"Mr. Booker?" Mack asked with more than just a question. "The Hall of Fame Groundskeeper?"

"Yes, Mack, the Hall of Famer," Billy laughed. You know about him?" Billy quizzed his teammate.

"Sure, I know about him," Mack said. "He's the only Groundskeeper in the Hall of Fame."

"Yep, he is," smiled Billy. He's been my Mentor since before I got on a travel squad. It was him who got me on my first travel baseball team," added Billy, appreciating Mr. Booker even more as Mack knew all about him.

"That's pretty cool, Billy. I'd have to think he knows as much about baseball as any manager today," laughed Mack.

"He knows more. He still follows every game and has watched me all season, hoping we'd get together over the break," said Billy. When I saw him a couple of weeks ago, he was prepared to tell me how I was going to break Ricky's record. I think he sees me as a player who can break Ricky's mark, and has pretty much groomed me to accomplish it."

"My gosh, Billy," Mack started. With Mr. Booker giving you advice since before you even got on a travel baseball squad, I'd have to think you just might do it."

"One more question, Billy, Mack started. "You are one of the few players in today's game that still wears metal spikes. Do you think that helps you?

Billy laughed as he told Mack the story about his first little league game, where the coach told him he could not wear metal spikes in that league, and how he was crying when he went back to the car to get his crummy rubber spikes.  When my Dad saw me crying, he asked why, and I explained what the coach had said.  I told him I didn't even want to play," Billy continued.

"Wow, I'm sure glad you changed your mind, but how long was it you had to wear the rubber spikes?" Mack asked.

"Mr. Booker came over one day with a brand new pair of metal spikes.  He explained the travel squads were allowed to wear them, and he'd already arranged a tryout for me." Billy remembered how much Mr. Booker had helped him in more ways than one.

"I had played with the same boys for a couple of years and didn't want to leave them," Billy said, as he remembered back to that one day in his life that probably changed his entire baseball career.  "When I got home and told my folks, they both quizzed me about leaving my friends. Then my mom spoke up and said, "Billy, after Bobby had to move away, you made new friends."

"What, you and Bobby knew each other as kids?" Mack was learning new things about his friend.

"He was my best friend for years.  Even after his Dad got transferred to Austin, Bobby and I would skype initially, until we both got iPhones, almost every night," Billy recounted. "We'd compare our stats, and Bobby would always lead me in HR's, but I'd always lead him in stolen bases."

So, why do you still wear your Metal Spikes when it seems most players are going to the plastic spikes because they are lighter," Mack asked and commented at the same time.

"They may be lighter, but I will never wear plastic spikes again. I'm a Metal Spikes guy, and always will be, "Billy laughed. "To be honest, I believe my Metal Spikes lets me get the speed that I have because they dig into the dirt better," continued Billy. "And of course, Ricky wore metal spikes." He laughed.

Mack said, "Well, I can't argue with that as you lead the league in steals this year. I think I'll start calling you MS for your metal spikes." Both boys laughed at that.

After dinner, they returned to the Hyatt Regency to get a good night's sleep before the next game, which was a day game. They had to be at the ballpark by 10:00 AM.

The Royals were on a hot streak and had been since the All-Star game. In the two remaining games against Cincy, the Royals won both by a good margin. Billy had four hits in the two games and stole three bases. He was now up to 43 stolen bases and pictured himself getting up to that magic 100 stolen bases that Ricky had his first full season.

# 15

## End Of Regular Season

It was now into the dog days of summer. August can be pretty hot in Kansas City, but not as hot as the Royals. They were on their way to winning the Central Division and, with a good finish, might reach a 100 win season. Billy was now hitting .315 and had 72 stolen bases to lead the league. He was the first player to get that many stolen bases by August 15th since Tom Scat had 70 bases to lead the league four years ago. He wore out in the last month and a half and only had ten stolen bases the rest of the way. Billy felt he could reach the 100 mark, but there were only 30 games left in the season. He wondered if he would wear out the same as Scat had done. He had to admit; he was tired.

In his first full season of playing 162 games, he was amazed at how tired and just plain worn out he felt. The traveling took it out of the players. All summer, they'd go from one road trip to another, one hotel after another. It was far more exhausting than Billy had ever imagined. So far, he'd played in every game, and was beginning to wonder if Coach Kessler might give him a day or two off. If the Coach did that, there would be no way Billy could reach 100 stolen bases.

In the next two series, Billy had a total of only four hits in six games. He stole each time he got on but was only up to 76 stolen bases with 20 games to go, and his batting average had dropped to .307.

His quest for 100 steals in his first full season came down to the last two series of the year, before the playoffs. He knew Ricky had reached 100 steals in the regular season. Oakland was not in the playoffs that year, or he might have stolen several more. The Royals were going to be in the playoffs, and Billy thought, "Maybe it will take the playoffs before I hit 100, but that wouldn't be the same as Ricky. Billy wanted to hit 100 in the regular season.

By now, Billy was up to 86 stolen bases, but with only two series left in the regular season, Billy started doubting if he could reach his goal. To do it, he had to steal 14 bases in six games. He figured it up and knew that he would only get up to bat 23-25 times in the last six games. That meant he almost had to get two hits a game and steal more bases, one for each of his hits, if he could do that.

The first series, the Royals won one and lost two. Billy was only up ten times. He had six hits and four stolen bases. So he was at 90 with three games to play.

All of a sudden, his bat went dead in the first game of the last series of the year. He struck out three times and hit a grounder back to the pitcher his last time up.

In the next game, he had two infield singles. He felt his bat was still dead, but his speed allowed him to beat out the throws on the two softly hit singles. Each time, the manager gave him the steal sign. Billy stole second base easily as he'd done all year. He hoped the manager would give him the sign to steal third, but it never happened.

It was the final game of the year. Billy needed nine steals in one game to reach Ricky's mark. He didn't even get a hit or a base on balls the entire game, so Billy Tankersly ended with 92 stolen bases, not enough to equal Ricky's 100 stolen bases his first year, but enough to lead the league by 20. He was disappointed, not even considering that he hit .302, which was the highest of any rookie in the American League. The playoffs wouldn't start for another three days, so Billy's folks drove him home. They had been at each of the Royals home games all season.

On the front porch of their house stood a beautiful blonde. Emma was there. Immediately, he forgot about not reaching Ricky's first-year mark. His folks laughed and said, "Surprise, Billy." He jumped out of the car and went running toward Emma, picking her up in his arms and feeling how good she felt to him.

"Am I being hugged by the guy that just led all of the major league in steals?" Emma laughed.

"I did?" Billy replied and asked. He was only following the steals by others in the American League and never even thought of the National League.

"Johnny Truman, the SS for San Diego only had 60, so you led all the major leagues," Emma told him, hugging him even tighter.

"If you have a first-half next year like you had the second half this year, you will be on the All-Star team, no way to keep you off," said Emma, already encouraging him for next year, and the Royals still had the playoffs ahead this year.

But right now, Billy was not thinking of the playoffs, or his 92 steals or anything other than Emma. Did you see the last game, Emma?" Billy asked.

"Of course, Billy. I knew you needed eight more steals to tie Ricky's first year, and even though that seemed impossible, I was there cheering you on, along with 42,000 others at Kaufman Stadium," she laughed. "The pressure on you in your own mind probably kept you from getting a hit today, but what a year my Billy Tankersly had," Emma said as they sat on the front porch in a new swing that his folks had bought since he'd been home last.

"Emma, I haven't even thought about it. As you can imagine....no, as you knew, I was so deep in my thoughts about getting to the 100 mark; I pretty much pushed everything else out of my mind.

"I noticed," said Emma, who hadn't heard from him for more than a month.

"Well, I can't even say, I'm sorry, Em.... I was so focused," Billy pouted.

"Hey, you've got three days before the playoffs start. Would you mind driving up to Lawrence with me tomorrow, just to explore KU more than I have so far?" Emma asked.

"That would be great," answered Billy, but right now, all he wanted was to eat dinner and go to bed. He was exhausted. He played in all 162 games, and he understood what Mr. Booker told him about the "dog days of summer." As much as he wanted to spend more time with Emma, he realized he was having a hard time even getting words out. He had no idea he'd be this tired.

The Tankersly's ate dinner with Emma, his Dad, and Mom doing most the talking. It was about him, but he just didn't care. He wanted to lay his head down on his own bed and snuggle up with his bat.

# <u>16</u>

## Attitude Can Change Everything

With Billy sleeping until 10:00, the first thing he noticed was his Mom holding a skillet with fried bacon by his bed. "Time to get up, sleepyhead," she said. Billy thought, "Mom, this is early for me, unless we're playing a day game," but he got up, put his sweats on, and remembered Emma was here. That got him to hurry to the kitchen table.

"Hey, buster, are we going to KU today or not?" Emma joked with the still-half-asleep Billy.

"Let me wake up first, "replied Emma's boyfriend.

After breakfast and Billy now wide-awake, they got in his folks' car and headed toward Lawrence which was only 30 miles up K-10 highway from their house.

As they entered Lawrence, Billy noticed that the city had changed since he was last there for a basketball game. After making a wrong turn, they finally saw the campus on top of Mt. Oread, the tallest point in Lawrence.

"Billy, I visited a lot of colleges in the past year, and KU is by far the prettiest campus," Emma said to Billy.

"So, what criteria did you use in choosing any college?" Billy asked.

"It was not finding the prettiest, but rather who had good sports management programs. Then it was talking to kids on campus, and figuring out where I felt I'd fit in the best," Emma continued. "It was interesting that it turned out to be the school closest to you, but that was not the main reason I chose KU, Billy. There was an attitude that I could feel on campus.....it was a winning attitude if that makes any sense at all," she said.

"It does, Em. I wanted to play for the Royals for the same reason. They had a winning attitude about them, even if they were losing," Billy added.

"I think we choose our friends the same way, or should anyway. We are normally around people that have a positive attitude rather than a negative one," Emma said. "I've watched you, Billy. I've seen you choose guys on the team that were cheerful and confident to be around. I also seen you avoid guys on the team that just had a negative attitude about everything."

"That is so true, Emma," continued Billy, fully engaged in the conversation. "I read in a book once that there was a survey of successful business people, and they were asked to rank four different categories about their success. The categories were IQ, Skills, Education, and Attitudes. It turned out that IQ, Skills, and Education only accounted for 7% of their success; 93% of their success was due to attitude," Billy added.

"Would that say to forget my education?" Emma asked.

Billy laughed because as soon as he told her what he had read, Billy knew he was pretty much saying, "forget your education, Emma."

"No, I think it's saying you have the attitude to get your education," Billy explained. "It's that attitude that many don't have....so I don't think in any way that survey was saying education is not important, but probably, you've got to have a certain attitude to get your education. But, once you've gotten your degree, in later life, no matter how successful you are, would fill out the survey the same way these business people did knowing it took a winning attitude even to seek getting a degree," Billy continued.

"Did that make any sense at all?" Billy asked.

"Sort of, Billy, you used a lot of words saying, "No, you are destined to be a KU Jayhawk.""

They both laughed, feeling like they were getting to know each other in a way they hadn't before.

"I read in a book called Think and Grow Rich, that you have to think positive," Emma said.

She continued, "it was cool because it pointed out the value of the thoughts that go through our heads, and how many ideas that pass by without any real thought given to them. The author said, "write all your thoughts down, because thoughts are things, and if written down, there's a chance you'll go back to them and get a deeper understanding of what you wrote down," Emma said. "After reading that book, I started writing down my thoughts about what I wanted out of life. Ultimately, that's what led me to KU. I wanted the best sports management program in the country because, like you, I want to be working for a major league baseball team."

"So we both have goals that no one else thinks we can reach," Billy laughed.

"Ain't that true, Billy Tankersly... who is going to break Ricky Henderson's stolen base record," Emma laughed along with the major leaguer.

"But that's back to our attitude, Emma. We believe we can achieve what we set out to achieve,"

Billy exclaimed. I think that's what those business people were saying. They had the attitude of believing, even before getting their education or creating whatever they might have created," said Billy to the girl sitting in the car with him, who was listening to his every word.

"You know, Billy, I'll bet you could have gotten straight A's at KU if you'd chosen that path. I think you'll succeed in breaking Ricky's record," Emma smiled as she leaned over and kissed him on his cheek.

"And I think you will be working for the Royals while I'm still playing with them," Billy confided in his new 'best friend.' "Would that be cool or what," Billly said with his voice already showing excitement like it was bound to happen. "Wait a minute," he continued. "Would that mean I'd be working FOR you?" he asked seriously. At least, Emma thought he was being serious.

"Yes sir, it would," Emma replied seriously. I would help manage the finances of the Royals, along with managing the marketing of the Royals, so you'd have to convince me you deserve a raise on your next contract. Part of my marketing would be marketing the players, you included."

"Gezzzz, I was joking," Billy said, really being serious now.

"So in Sports Management, you manage?" Billy asked, learning more and more about her education.

"Yep, Mr. Tankersly. I will be determining your future with the Royals," she laughed.

"Guess I'd better get close to you then, eh?" Billy smiled. "So show me the classrooms you'll be studying in," Billy suggested.

They parked the car and started walking around the main campus. She took him into the Student Union, and then out on the patio overlooking the new KU football stadium. It looked to Billy to be as nice as the one in Austin; he'd seen as he had driven past the University of Texas. Then they took the student bus over to the basketball area, which included Phog Allen Fieldhouse, where Billy had seen many Jayhawk games with his Dad.

Emma showed him something he'd never seen; another part of the Fieldhouse that was new. It was where the original rules of basketball were housed in a case on the wall that no one could break.

"One of the KU alumni purchased the original rules written by James Naismith, the founder of basketball," she told Billy.

He thought he remembered telling her about James Naithsmith before, but maybe she did not know that he was buried right across the street from Allen Fieldhouse. He thought he'd catch her on that.

"Do you know where he's buried, Emma?" Billy asked.

"That's a crazy question, Billy," she replied. "Why in the world would I know where a man was buried, and why would I want to know anyway?"

"Well, it's sort of important because it tells you that less than a block away, he was so important to KU that they made a special cemetery just for him," Billy explained.

"OK, you got me on that one," laughed Emma. "I had no idea about that."

It has been a fun afternoon, as they got in the car and headed back to KC.

That night, Billy went to bed early, preparing for his early morning workout the next day at Kauffman.

# <u>17</u>

## Practice Before The First Playoff Game

Billy woke with his bat by his side. He felt good when getting out of bed. Then he smelled the bacon and was ready to start the day, as he carried his bat to the kitchen. He hugged his Mom and Emma and shook his Dad's hand, telling him to watch his son steal three bases tomorrow in the first game of the playoffs. Because the Royals had the best record in baseball, they would have the advantage of being the home team in each series if they won.

Emma took Billy to the stadium. As he got out of the car, he leaned over and kissed her. "You are my good luck charm," he smiled.

"How long will your practice session be today, Billy?" Emma asked.

"I'm guessing that Coach Kessler only wants us to loosen up, take a few grounders on infield practice, and then hit for probably five to ten minutes. "If we are hitting the ball squarely, Coach will probably let us hit just enough to get loose," Billy added. I don't know if they will let you in for the practice as I imagine it will be a closed practice where even the reporters are barred.

"Come back in two hours," Billy told or asked Emma. He didn't mean for it to come out like an order, but it did, nonetheless.

"I'll see you then, Billy," Emma responded, not taking Billy's comment as an order.

Billy walked into the clubhouse, and Mack and Bobby were already suited up.

"Hey, Tank, practice is over, you were suppose to be here at 8:00 AM," Bobby said to his best friend. "I think Coach is upset that you didn't make it on time. Maybe you'd better go into his office to apologize, to not get in more trouble."

Billy walked into Coach Kessler's office, and his first words were, "Billy, I'm glad you are early. I wanted to discuss something with you," Coach Kessler said. Billy was confused. Had his best friend just pulled another joke on him? He finally figured out that was the case, and he had to smile as Coach told him that he wanted him to focus on getting on base. "Billy, we are going to run every chance we get. I know you didn't hit the 100 stolen bases you were shooting for in the regular season, but if we can win the first five game series against the Angels, you should have enough games left to shatter that 100 imaginary goal you set," the coach added.

"Why did you say "imaginary" goal, Coach?" Billy asked.

"Because you've got an entire career to beat Ricky's record," Coach Kessler said as he put his arm around Billy. "Do you know how many stolen bases Ricky got his second year?" the coach asked Billy.

"No, coach, I just know he had 100 his first full year," Billy replied."

"Well, if you'd looked closer, you would have found out that he only stole 56 bases his second full year, and yet he hit .303. He was thrown out 22 times," the Kansas City skipper added. "Granted, his third year, he stole 130 while only hitting .257, but if you have as good a year next year as you've had this year, you will be far ahead of Ricky by the time you start your third year. Now, I want to see you steal ten bases this first series," Coach Kessler said to Billy.

Billy was taking it all in. He didn't know why he hadn't looked at what Ricky did his second full year. "From what the coach just told me, I stand a real good chance of being ahead of Ricky by my third year," Billy thought to himself as he left the Coaches office.

Bobby was still at his locker talking to Mack, and both boys laughed at Billy's as they were sure they'd pranked him. They could just imagine the fear Billy had walking into the coach's office, thinking he'd missed the practice. "We got you on that one, Billy," Mack said, laughing his fanny off.

"Yeah, you guys got me good. I was scared to death to walk into the coach's office, thinking I'd missed the entire practice. All sorts of things were going through my mind, with the main one being, "I'm not going to start tomorrow." Mack and Bobby laughed even harder. "We gotcha Tank."

Billy suited up, hit the field, knowing he was going to have a good practice session. Within five minutes, the coach was on the field with them, as the players were just playing catch with each other, loosing up.

The coach gathered everyone together. "Guy's, I don't want to put pressure on you, but the Angels will wilt under our pitching and offense and speed. I told Billy earlier that I expected him to steal ten bases in this first series, and that goes for each of you. Maybe ten stolen bases is out of the question for some of you, like Bobby, who is going to drive all of you in with probably five HR's this series. Still, the point is, we are going to play a speed game this series, which means more bunting, more hitting to the opposite field, more running out every ground ball as hard as you can run, in hopes their infielders will throw the ball away, trying to hurry their throws. Just expect a hit and run type game," the coach concluded.

Infield practice was only 15 minutes long, and Billy made one hard play after another. He and Mack worked on their double play situations, and they had played so long together, in the minors and now in the majors, that they knew what the other was going to do before he even did it. Mack knew the throws from Billy would be chest-high, no matter where the ball was hit. Billy knew the same about Mack, chest-high throws to Billy where he could tag the base and have the ball transferred from his glove to his throwing arm in a split second, and then a bullet to first base.

Infield practice was good as it got everyone back to thinking about nothing but winning the first playoff series.

Hitting practice was the same for Billy. He was hitting line-drives all over the field with a velocity of over 100 mph hour on each of his hits. He knew he could increase his homers next year by just adjusting his bat slightly. He wanted to hit singles though so he could steal bases, but hearing that Ricky also led all leadoff batters in home runs made him want to increase his strength over the winter.

Practice was less than an hour, but each of the players felt it had been a good workout, especially since it was still warm in KC with 70 degree days, perfect for the players and the fans. They knew there would be 42,613 fans yelling from the first pitch to the last. Kansas City always had a great fan base, and the entire city was excited about the upcoming series.

Billy walked outside after changing out of his uniform, and there was Emma, with the music in the car turned up full blast. Unlike most guys his age, he didn't keep up with the latest songs, and he didn't recognize the song coming from the car.

"What group was that?" Billy asked, as soon as Emma turned it down, seeing Billy walking toward her.

"It is the greatest group since the Beatles, Billy. Have you ever heard of the Skywalkers?" she asked.

"Nope," he confessed. Emma just laughed. "If it had been a song about Billy Tankersly stealing another base, I'll bet you'd know them."

Billy laughed and replied in a cocky way, "When I steal my 1407th base, maybe they will write a song about the speedster Billy Tankersly," he laughed as he got in the car for the 25-minute drive home.

# <u>18</u>

## Royals Play The Angels

The game started with Butch Kelly throwing nothing but strikes.  He was hitting the target that Bucky Walters set on each pitch.  Billy knew the Angels were not going to hit Butch, the way he was throwing. He'd never been a pitcher who threw 100 mph, but he hit the corners one pitch after another, and the Angels went down in order in the first inning.

Coach Kessler changed the batting order with Billy leading off.  He knew why.....the coach wanted to give him every chance to get on base and start the running game.  With Mack hitting second, he had proven all year long to be a good hit and run hitter, hitting behind the baserunner.  He also knew to take a pitch when Billy was on base because it was likely that "Tank" would be barreling down on the 2nd baseman or the SS, whichever one was covering on steal situations.  Just like the Royals, the Angels had scouted the Royals and already knew it would be a running game for the K.C. team.

Billy took the first pitch to him, wanting to see what "Flagstaff Baines" would throw him.  Since the Angels were in the West Division, they didn't get to play each other very often, but everyone knew if Billy got on, he would end up at second base.

The pitch was a four-seam fastball that hit 97 mph hour on the radar guns, and it had a late break to it.  Billy knew after one pitch that he could hit him.

On the second pitch, Billy hit a line drive in the gap between center and left field.  No one could get to it, and Billy headed to second.  As the play was in front of him, he saw the centerfielder juggle the ball just for a second.  He headed to third.  The throw arrived at 3B, but the Royals speedster was already there.  The dugout and the fans were cheering so loudly; Billy had a hard time hearing the third base coach prompt him on what Mack was going to do.  Billy thought he saw the bunt sign but wasn't positive.  It was a situation if Billy had called time to talk to the coach to make sure he heard him right or read the sign correctly, it would be a dead giveaway to the Angels, so Billy took a good size lead anticipating a squeeze play.

All of a sudden, Flagstaff was throwing to third to try to pick him off.  It would have worked if Billy hadn't been prepared.   The instant he realized Flagstaff's feet shifted slightly, Billy knew he was going to try to pick him off, so he started running toward home.  The third baseman for the Angels fired a strike to the Angels catcher.  It was close, but Billy saw the umpires arms spread, so he knew he'd beaten the thrown.  There was no way he could hear the umpire say "safe" as the fans at Kauffman were on their feet yelling at the top of their lungs. All 42,000 plus fans in attendance were waving blue towels with "Royals Forever" printed on them that they received as they entered Kauffman Stadium.  Flagstaff had only thrown two pitches and was trailing 1-0.  Immediately, he seemed to lose his confidence, walking Mack on four pitches.  Arturo was hitting third, and he walked on four straight pitches, not even close to the plate.  The Angels pitching coach walked to the mound, attempting to settle his pitcher down.  Bobby was now at the plate, and the Angels knew Bobby Barns could hit one out of Kauffman. Everyone on the Royals knew Flagstaff would throw a curve on his first pitch to Bobby. Flagstaff was so concerned about the batter that he didn't notice Mack and Arturo taking larger leads than normal. As his leg crossed the rubber, the two Royals were off and running to steal two more bases. They were both fast, not as fast as Billy, but fast enough to steal bases. So, with first base open, the catcher walked to the mound to ask Flagstaff if he would rather put Bobby on 1B with an intentional walk or pitch to him. The two agreed to pitch to Bobby.

Wrong decision, as Bobby hit one over the centerfield fence for a three-run homer on the first pitch. The fans were yelling even louder than on Billy's hit. It was so loud that as Bobby crossed the plate to be greeted by his teammates, he couldn't hear what they were saying. Kansas City fans had a pent-up desire to see the Royals reach and win the World Series, and the start of this game gave them the confidence that this was the Royals year as the team had 4-0 lead and Flagstaff had only thrown a total of 10 pitches.

He kicked the dirt behind the mound. He did not want to see the pitching coach or manager come out to the mound again. He started hitting the corners like he had all year, striking the next three Royals out, two on called third strikes.

Butch set the Angels down in the second without a hit. He was sharp today. The Royals didn't score again until the 6th when Billy led off. In his second time up, he'd hit a line drive directly at the 1B, so he was now 1 for 2, with no stolen bases, not counting his steal of home.

He took the first pitch, which was called a strike. Flagstaff had not given up a hit since that first inning. He knew he could not give Billy a good enough pitch to hit, but he didn't want to walk him either. The next pitch was a curve, and again, Billy watched it cross the outside corner for a strike. With a 0-2 count, there was no way Billy would not be swinging on anything close to the plate. He fouled off the next five pitches, and Flagstaff was shaken up by that. No matter whether he threw a curve or fastball on the outside or inside, Billy was getting wood on it even if each ball hit had been foul. The young SS was now expecting a fastball as he was pretty sure Flagstaff did not want to walk him. The pitch was down the middle, and Billy swung. The ball traveled 413 feet and ended up in the right field stands. Billy had his first HR in the playoffs, and the score was now 5-0. The cheering was once again so loud that he couldn't understand what his teammates were saying as he crossed the plate.

He did hear Bobby as he put his arm on Billy's shoulder. "Hey, Tank, I'm the one who is supposed to hit HRs. You are supposed to hit singles so you can steal, remember?" Bobby razzed his best friend.

That was the end of the scoring for both teams. The Royals had won, 5-0 in the first game of the five game series. Of course, if the Royals won the next two games, the series would be over with the Royals playing the Chicago White Sox for the American League championship. Billy did have a chance in the 8th inning to get on again, and maybe steal a base or two, but he hit a long fly ball to the right fielder, so he ended with two hits, a triple and HR. Not bad for a 19-year-old kid, he thought to himself, smiling. He` was still smiling as he and Bobby walked out of the clubhouse to be met by Emma. Bobby hugged her before Billy could even say hi to her. Billy knew if he had not asked Bobby not to ask her out while in Lexington, she'd probably be with Bobby now because he admitted to Billy that he wanted to ask her out. Instead, they just became good friends, and Billy was not jealous at all, with Bobby hugging Emma. Emma told Billy the day they went fishing that she liked Bobby, and if she wasn't so madly in love with Billy, she might have asked him out. Billy just laughed at the time, thinking that Bobby would always be Emma's best friend because both had a good time together. Then she turned and gave Billy a big kiss, telling him what a great game he had just played. He felt good. His folks, standing aside, were happy for their son.

The second game was much tighter than the first game, with the Angels scoring the first run. Billy flied out to the centerfielder his first time up. It was now the fourth inning, and Billy was leading off. He saw they had the 3rd baseman on the 1B side of second in a shift more pronounced than other times up. The SS was closer to second base than he was third base. Billy wondered if they expected him to pull the ball that much. He made up his mind. He was going to lay a drag bunt down the third baseline. On the second pitch, a changeup over the outside of the plate, Billy laid down a perfect bunt. There wasn't even a throw to first base. On the first pitch to Mack, Billy took off for second base. He arrived much sooner than the catcher's throw. Billy had his second stolen base in the playoffs. Unfortunately, Mack struck out, so it was up to Arturo to bring him home.

Flagstaff knew Billy might try to steal third. Before throwing a pitch, he twirled around and faked a throw to second, trying to keep Billy close to the bag. The second time he turned around, he threw it to the SS, who had tried to sneak in behind Billy, but he was back in plenty of time.

When the Angels hurler finally threw a pitch to Arturo, Billy was off like a bullet, sliding into third with another stolen base. Flagstaff was furious at himself and more determined than ever to keep Billy from scoring. With only one out, Flagstaff knew a fly ball would score Billy with the tying run. On the third pitch to him, Arturo hit a ground ball straight back to the pitcher. He checked Billy at third and threw a strike to their first baseman. Flagstaff won that battle but still had to face Bobby Bonds. Since there were now two outs, he was a little relieved and knew he just had to get Bonds out.

Bobby took two pitches, one a ball and one a strike. On the third pitch, he hit a hard line drive into the left-field corner for a double, scoring Billy easily to tie the game, 1-1.

The Angel's manager walked slowly to the mound. He raised his left arm that meant the lefty reliever; Sam Boyce, was coming in. Flagstaff gave him the ball, grudgingly.

Boyce was one of the best middle relievers in baseball. He threw a fastball that reached 100 mph and a changeup that only hit 75 mph on the radar gun. He was hard to hit.

Terrance, batting 5th, hit the second pitch over the third baseman's outstretched glove for a single, scoring Bobby with the lead run. Jackson hitting 6th this game, kept the rally going with a hit over second base for a single. Terrance had to stop at 2B, but Christian Louis, the catcher batting 7th, kept the rally going with a seeing-eye ground ball between the SS and 3B that scored Terrance with the third run of the inning.  That was the end of the scoring, but the Royals now led 3-1.

Like in the first game, neither team scored in the late innings, and the Royals now had a two-game lead but were going to Los Angeles, the home of the Angels, for the next two games, or one game if the Royals won.

There was a travel day before the first game at the Angels Stadium.  Billy hugged Emma, his folks, and Mr. Booker, who came to the second game.  Billy noticed he was not at the first game, and Billy asked if he was feeling OK?  He thought to himself that Mr. Booker looked much older.  All of them were happy for Billy's start in the playoffs.  In the first two games, Billy had three stolen bases, a HR, and several brilliant plays at SS.

Before getting on the flight, Billy was saying good-bye to his fan club of Emma, Billy's folks, and Mr. Booker, who came with Mr. and Mrs. Tankersly to the game.  He missed the first one because of just not feeling good enough to go. Billy thought Mr. Booker had aged  20 years since Billy last saw him. The Royals SS  made a point to hug Mr. Booker and thank him for all the training he had given him.

"Mr. Booker, I would not be here if not for you," Billy started.  "All the time you spent with me, pushing me to be better, is why I'm playing for the Royals," Billy concluded as he hugged Mr. Booker a little tighter.  Mr. Booker smiled, but not a word out of his mouth.  That made Billy wonder just how bad Mr. Booker's health was.

# <u>19</u>

## Off To Los Angeles

On the flight, Billy's mind was on Mr. Booker. The man had been like a second father to him, and Billy was concerned about his health. The entire team was on this flight, making Billy think about others, including an entire women's soccer team, who had died when a flight went down.

All of a sudden, it was like checking his attitude and realizing that his worrying was burning a lot of energy. He remembered reading "worrying burns energy while not worrying stores energy." In his first two years of playing professional baseball, Billy had seen how worrying did burn a lot of energy. He made up his mind to think only about the game in front of him, not Mr. Booker or missing Emma. Mack and Bobby were in the same row as Billy, and the three of them began talking about the Angels game and LA.

"Hey Bobby, ya think we can beat them in the first game to claim the Division title and a chance to play for the American League title?" Billy asked his best bud.

"Well, if we win our Division Title, it's a sure bet we'll be playing the White Sox for the American League championship. The White Sox, who started the playoffs a day before the Royals, had beaten the Astro's three straight games and were already in the League championship. That extra day allowed them to watch the Royals playing the Angels. Because they'd played each other during the regular season, they probably would not see anything they hadn't seen before. However, Coach Kessler might change the pitching rotation, throwing Roger Doxee, who they had not seen. Roger was like a 5th starter but had an exceptional changeup that would get hitters swinging at pitches that bounced in the dirt in front of the plate.

As the plane started it's descent toward the LA airport, Billy looked out the window and saw nothing but lights as far as he could see. He remembered playing out there during the regular season, but for some reason, he had no idea just how large L.A. was. The plane landed right on time. As the players got off the plane, they were thankful a team of the office personnel collected all the Royals' luggage. That allowed the team to go directly to the hotel and meet in the hotel restaurant for dinner.

Over dinner, Coach Kessler made it a point to walk around the tables, talking to each player. When he approached Billy, he put his hands on Billy's shoulder.

"Billy, you've had a great series so far, and I still want you to steal whenever you've got the opposing pitcher measured. You have my permission to steal, even if we have not given you a steal sign," the coach told him. Billy was proud, or at least happy, that the coach had that much confidence in him.

After dinner, a couple of the older guys went to the bar, but Billy and Bobby were still too young to drink. They headed to their rooms, not talking about much. Billy's thoughts were about the upcoming game and how, with a win, the Royals would win the Division title. He went to sleep with his bat on the other side of the bed.

The game was a night game, and since there was two hours difference between KC and West Coast time, the game started at 7:10 PM, which was 9:10 KC time. Billy wondered if the time difference would affect the team. It turned out; it didn't make any difference at all as the Royals took the third game of the series, just as easy as the games in Kansas City. The Royals were now going to face the Chicago White Sox for the American League Pennant. The flight home was fun as the players stood by others remaining in their seats, all talking about the past series. Now and then, one of the players would yell, "Bring on the Sox," and others would yell back, "Those Sox smell." Then another would yell, "American League Champions, the Kansas City Royals."

The plane landed, and thousands of fans were outside the Kansas City Airport, cheering like they were at a game already. As the players got off, there were cheers for each player. When Bobby got off, it was like another level or cheering. Finally, Billy got off. The crowd was waiting for their hometown success story player. They cheered and cheered even louder with many held signs that said, "Beat the Sox, and Billy, steal another base." The KC fans had waited many years for successful teams, and once again, just like the last three years, they were going for an American League Pennant. Unfortunately, they didn't have a World Series Championship yet, but the Royals were the odds on favorite to beat the WhiteSox and get back to the World Series again.

Billy saw his Dad, Mom, Emma, and Mr. Booker waiting outside the gates. He couldn't run because of players in front of him, but he wanted to do just that.  As soon as he reached them, he hugged his Mom, then his Dad and Mr. Booker, and finally Emma.  Each was a special hug because it was these people who had helped him be successful.  Even Emma had helped him in the past two years.

"Well," said his Dad, "it seems you've had a pretty good year, Billy."

Billy replied, "Dad, winning is everything, but you've watched me keep stats all my life, and I know exactly what I did this year."  Mr. Tankersly laughed and quizzed his son, "what was your on-base stat this year?"  ".364," replied Billy.  They all laughed, and finally, it was Billy who said, "do you know how many bases I've stolen so far?"

His Dad, Mom, Mr. Booker, and Emma, all at once said, "96".  All Billy could do was smile as he remembered, in a split second, almost every base he did steal.  Everyone else was laughing that they all knew it was 96.

"Thanks to Mr. Booker, who got me to take a bigger lead off the base," you all are right," Billy confided in everyone on the drive home.  "OK, I know if it had been 67, you all would have gotten that right too, but Mr. Booker shared some things with me over the All-Star break about Ricky Henderson," explained Billy.  "One was to set a goal every day of how many I would steal, which meant keeping my eye on the ball until it hit my bat each time up, so I could get on base to steal," added Billy, wanting Mr. Booker to know how much he had helped Billy.

Billy sat in the back seat with Mr. Booker and Emma on the ride home. Kansas City looked so good. The trees had already changed their color, and the leaves were starting to fall. Billy said, "Hey, Dad.  I have not forgotten the Fall season in KC, and what I remember the most about it."

"What was that, Billy?" his Dad asked.

"You making me rake all those stupid leaves off the yard," Billy laughed.

Mr. Tankersly always had a comeback for Billy. "It was teaching you that we all have responsibilities."

"Yeah, yeah, yeah, it was because you had a son who could do it for you," Billy laughed again, this time at his humor. He knew it was one of the lessons of life that his Dad had taught him, and he was thankful. Billy was thinking to himself about having to mow yards each summer to get spending money and then stashing it all in a savings account. He was grateful that his Dad had taught him that lesson. As a major leaguer with a sizeable monthly income, he had to have a money manager help him with his investments. But the teachings of his youth remained with him.

Heck, it didn't take a lot of money on the road because the team gave each player an allowance for food, haircuts, etc. Billy didn't even spend all of that, as he watched every penny he was spending. A ballplayer never knew how long his career would be, but Billy, even with all his dreams, knew that the average for a rookie starting his first season would only last 5.6 years. With better health, training, and higher salaries since 2000, the percentage jumped up to 8.2 years.

Billy realized that he'd been into his thoughts and asked Emma how her schooling was going.

"Billy, we've only been in classes for three weeks," answered Emma. Billy stayed on Emma.

"OK, three weeks...., so how do you like KU?" he asked. She laughed and said, "are you envious?"

"Yeah, that's it, Em, I'm envious," said Billy, not even with a smile. "I know you think I'm joking, but in all my young years, I just imagined I'd be a Jayhawk," he explained. "So you are getting the life I expected to have," continued Billy.

"Well, Billy, I always imagined I'd be a major league SS," laughed Emma, "so I guess we don't always get what we want."

"Hey kiddo, I am going to get what I want....1408 stolen bases at the end of my career," Billy said seriously.

By now, they were all sitting in Billy's living room, and when he said that, a cheer broke out from all of them. "Go, Billy, Go."

# <u>20</u>

## American League Championship Series

As it had been in the Division Playoffs, the Royals had the home-field advantage against the White Sox. It was important because if the series were tied after four games, the final game would be at Kauffman Stadium.

The players were warming up before the game, and the stands were already full. The noise was almost ear-shattering. Everyone was cheering, and the game hadn't even started.

At 7:05 PM, the Royals took the field, and the crowd was going wild in appreciation and hoping to help the Royals win the first game. The game-time temperature was 77 degrees. Perfect for the players and the fans.

Butch Kelly had earned the right to start the first game, and he struck out the White Sox in order in the first inning. Billy was leading off again, meaning the coach was expecting the game to be one where Billy got on base and stole bases. Nothing could rattle an opposing pitcher more than to have the leadoff batter get on base and then steal.

The White Sox pitcher was Tommy Donk and was known for his fastball. He hit 100 mph almost every game.

Billy stepped into the box, to the roar of the Kansas City crowd. He expected a fastball on the first pitch since that was Donk's starting pitch in most games. He got it right over the heart of the plate, and Billy didn't get the bat off his shoulder.

"Strike One," yelled the umpire.  Billy was surprised that he had not noticed who the umpire was before he stepped up to the plate.

"Come on, ump, get some eyes," Billy yelled as he turned around to razz  Art Brown who was the first umpire to congratulate Billy in his first time at the plate last year.  "Hey Hotshot, you'd better not object too much, or I'll throw you out of the game," shouted Ump Brown over the noise of the crowd. Billy remembered, "Hot Shot" was what Art Brown called him his first game in the majors.  "Yeah, Yeah, Yeah," laughed Billy as he turned around to face Donk again.  He expected another fastball.

He knew he had to "soften" his bat for what he intended to do.  He realized that third base was almost vacant as the White Sox were playing him to pull.  He turned to bunt, pulled the bat back just a little to slow the bunt to where it didn't even reach third base.  The ball did precisely what Billy was visualizing.  It died before it reached the bag, and no one was able to reach it before Billy was past first base.  He had his first hit of the game and was expecting to see the steal sign on the first pitch to Mack, who again was hitting second.

Billy had never faced Donk, so he didn't know his pickoff moves.  Coach Keller knew that and did not give Billy the steal sign of the first pitch.  Billy remembered Mr. Booker's instructions. "Take a lead of 11 to 12 feet".  He did just that, and sure enough, Donk threw quickly to the first baseman.  Billy slid and knew he was safe.  Now he'd seen one of Donk's pickoff moves, but was sure he had a faster one, so he took a 10-foot lead, bounced up and down like he was going to run, and Donk threw to first again, only this time, it was much faster than his first pickoff move. Because Billy had adjusted his lead to only 10 feet, he slid again but could have stood up getting back. He wanted to put as much pressure on Donk as he could, and the fans were loving it, cheering wildly each time Billy got back in time.

Now it was time to steal, even though he had not yet thrown one pitch to Mack. He looked to the third base coach, and there he was, was rubbing his letters, touching his left arm with two fingers and a bunch of other signs, that meant nothing. It seemed Billy always knew the pitcher's mind. He knew the coach on third saw exactly what had happened and gave Billy the sign he wanted. Billy bolted, using his metal spikes to dig into the dirt that propelled him. "Safe," yelled the ump as Billy slid into second base.

"What a thrill," Billy thought. "Being able to play in an American League championship in front of his home town fans." His thoughts immediately returned to the game as Mack hit one in the gap, scoring Billy. The KC fans were on their feet, yelling as loud as Billy had ever heard. The next few batters were already on the steps of the dugout, running out to greet Billy, were yelling loud enough that Billy could hear, "Way to go, Billy."

Arturo was up next, and he wasted no time in driving one off the left-field wall at the "K," which was the nickname for Kauffman Stadium. He stopped at first base because the ball was hit so hard, it bounced right into the left fielder's hands, and Mack had to go back to second base. Bobby was next up with runners on first and second.

The fans roared as Bobby had become a "hometown" hero like Billy since he was born here.

Billy watched him tip his hat. "What a ham," Billy thought.

Bobby took the count to 3 & 2 before walking. Now the Royals had the bases loaded with no outs.

Terrace Moore was batting 5th as he had in all the series games. He, like Bobby, had power, and the White Sox pitching coach walked to the mound to remind him that Terrance could also hit a HR. As he walked back to the dugout, he'd no sooner turned around to the field to see Terrance lace a fastball into the right field corner, clearing the bases. The Royals were up 4-0, and like other games where the Royals had gotten off to a fast a start, the White Sox pitching coach walked to the mound again, but this time two relief pitchers were warming up in the bullpen. Finally, the umpire came out to break up the "meeting." Everyone knew he was trying to give the guys in the bullpen extra seconds to get warm. He ambled back to the dugout, giving the bullpen even more time to get warm.

Jackson Triade was anxious to hit against Donk after seeing what the first five batters had done. The first pitch was so high; the catcher had to reach as high as he could to keep it from going back to the backstop. "Ball one," signaled the ump. Jackson was disappointed to see the manager walk to the mound this time. That meant for sure that Donk was being pulled. Sure enough, in walked Spike Tipila, who was known to be a long reliever. He started several games for the Sox during the regular season. Billy didn't need to look at what he'd done on a computer like the manager. He knew Spike threw three main pitches. A fastball, curve, and cutter.

Spike's first pitch to Jackson was a fastball. Billy wished he'd been at the plate. It looked like a meatball. The ump signaled "Strike One." Jackson, like Billy, knew the first pitch from Spike to him would be a fastball since he had one ball on him before Spike came in. He had to get Jackson out. But he let it go by, just to be able to judge just how effective Spike would be. Jackson was a patient hitter, so the White Sox reliever was going to have to throw strikes. He didn't on the next pitcher, and now the count was 2-1.

Everyone in the park knew that Tipila would throw a fastball down the heart of the plate. Jackson was ready. He swung and missed. As he gave himself a dirty look, if that's possible, everyone in the stands saw it. The count was now 2-2. Tipila had no room to waste a pitch. He had to come back with one he felt could get Jackson out. It was a cutter that broke down and almost hit the plate, but the ump yelled, "Stike Three." All Jackson could do was turn around and question the umpire, "just where was that pitch." The umpire didn't even bother to answer Jackson.

As Aaron Troupe stepped into the batter's box, with Christian Louis, the catcher batting after Aaron, it was obvious that Spike Tipila had a little more confidence now after striking out Jackson.

He struck out Aaron on three pitches. Christian was known for his catching ability, not his hitting, and Tipila struck Christian out on four pitches to end the inning. The Royals led by four.

Billy got up in the second inning right after Alex Hart, the Dher. Alex led off with a double. Billy was disappointed to see a bunt sign from the third-base coach.  He knew that was the right move, having a man on third base with only one out.  He didn't try to get a base hit out of his bunt as it was a true sacrifice bunt.  The pitcher threw him out, but Alex was able to get to third. Mack and Arturo struck out to end the inning.  The entire momentum of the game seemed to change right then.  No one ever knows why, when, or how, but the momentum was on the side of the White Sox.  They scored in the next three innings, a total of five runs to lead the game, and the Royals never scored another run.  Billy was 1-3 with one stolen base.  The Royals trailed in a playoff series for the first time in two years.

# <u>21</u>

## American League Series Continues

The second game at the "K" was no different than the first game.  The Royals got a lead, only to see it overtaken in the 6th inning. Tom Crawfish, one of the recent call-ups, got beat up for six runs.  The Royals never recovered.  Billy was 2-4 with one stolen base, but what did it matter?  The final score of the second game was 10-3.  Now the Royals were going to Chicago to play in XTRSX Field, which long ago was named Comiskey Park before sponsors paid for the naming rights.  The park hadn't changed, just the name of the park.  Billy didn't know if the naming of the parks was a bidding process or what, but the parks sure seem to change names a lot.  All except the "K."

There was a day off before the series resumed. Most of the players flew to Chicago and stayed in a hotel. Billy's parents and Emma asked Billy if he could stay at home since it was a day off.  He didn't think twice.  "No, I should stay with the team; they need some confidence-building right night, and I can do that," Bill concluded before kissing and hugging everyone good-bye as he boarded the team plane to Chicago.

He and Mack were sitting across the aisle from each other.  They talked about the fact they needed to get on base since they were batting first and second.

"Hey, Mack," Billy said loud enough for his voice to carry about six rows in front and six in back.  "We are going to win the next two games and bring it back to Kansas City. We owe it to the fantastic fans that have come out to see us all year," Billy tried to cheer and motivate the team.

"You can say that again, Billy," shouted Bobby. "We are going to bring it home and win the series in KC."

Several of the rest of the team shouted out something positive, and it was a good flight to Chicago. Billy felt he'd made the right decision in flying with the team.

The next day, Bobby and Billy explored Chicago. They came to a place called the Miracle Mile, or something like that. At least, that's what Bobby called it. No matter, it was a miracle of high-end shops for close to a mile, if it wasn't a full mile. Neither of them was interested, so they just started exploring. The Royals rented a car for Billy since he was not old enough to rent one himself. The friends saw beautiful churches right in the middle of a neighborhood. The homes looked expensive in that neighborhood. Then they went to North Avenue Beach on Lake Michigan. They took their shoes off, rolled their pants up, and walked into Lake Michigan for about two seconds.

"Holy Smokes, Bobby, that is the coldest water I've ever felt," shouted Billy. "Hey Billy, ya gotta remember, I'm the guy who got to live in Austin only 100 miles from the beach," Bobby laughed, "and this was COLD!"

They drove through downtown looking up at the enormous buildings. Bobby said, "Austin is starting to look like this." Billy just glared up at one tall building after another. After the two major league ballplayers grabbed a bite to eat, Bobby said, " let's head back to the hotel and see if any of the guys are in the lounge talking about the game." Billy thought to himself, "Bobby has turned into a leader, as he is leading me."

No one was in the lounge as the other players had already gone to their rooms to get a good night's sleep. Billy did not sleep alone. He had his bat. He woke with one hand on the bat, like he'd been swinging all night long.

The team met briefly before the game was to start. Coach Kessler, once again, not trying to put pressure on the team, but he couldn't resist, "Guys, it's do or nothing tonight....a win and we get to play tomorrow night. A loss, and we will have a long winter."

Chicago at this time of the year can be bitter cold, but fortunately, the weather tonight was warm. The teams warmed up in the late afternoon and had a team meeting before the game. Coach Kessler got the team together, saying, "Let's hustle out every play and win this game."

The Royals were the visitors, so they batted first. Billy swung the "At Bat" bat that had a heavy ring on it, that made his real bat light. When he got to the plate, he felt excited and ready to win this game for sure.

He took two balls before getting one he could hit, and it was on the outside corner, so he hit it to left field. The outfielders did not go into the same shift that the infielders used. The ball dropped in front of the left fielders for a hit. The Chicago crowd did not roar like the "K" fans would have. Mack was batting second, and he knew to give Billy the chance to steal second.  The first pitch was over the heart of the plate, and Billy didn't even break for second base. Mack looked at Billy like, "what the heck, buddy?"

Billy knew he did not have a good read on Foster, the pitcher for the Sox.  On the second pitch, he was ready.  He ran, and Mack swung.  He hit a sharp grounder to the SS that resulted in a double play.  "Doggone it, Billy, I wish you'd gone on the first pitch," Mack thought to himself.

Arturo hit a long fly ball to centerfielder, but not long enough to get out of the park or avoid being caught.  Three up, three down.

Art Holmes was pitching the third game for the Royals.  A win for the Sox here would stop the Royals from reaching the World Series.  After losing last year in the 7th game of the American League Championship, it had been their goal all year long to get back to that point and then win the World Series.

Now they were two games from not reaching their goal.  They had to win the first game in Chicago and then a second game to get back to Kansas City. Art struck out the first batter, Henry Gonzalez, on a wicked change-up.  He looked good.  The second batter rolled a soft grounder to Billy, who threw him out in plenty of time.  Groucho Tallis was the third hitter for the White Sox this game since Art was a lefty.  Groucho was known as a power hitter when he got to play.  He was a right-handed batter and only got to face lefties for most of the season.  There was a good reason for the White Sox management to play Groucho this way.....he hit .346 against lefties in the regular season, while hitting only .138 against right-handed pitchers.  "Art is not going to throw him anything good," Billy thought.

He was right.  Groucho walked on four pitches.

With a runner on first, Mack and Billy talked, via signs, who was going to take the throw on a steal. There were other signs between them on who was going to shift, along with about a dozen other options in deciding where to play the batter, Frzzo Abrams, the cleanup batter this game.  This was the first time Frzzzo had batted cleanup since August 23rd.  Billy had no idea since Frizzo didn't have a hit in the first two games.  Billy was thinking, "this Frizzzo guy didn't even play in the first two games, and now he's hitting cleanup?

Before thinking any more, Frizzo hit a grounder to Mack, who threw to 1st for the third out, and now it was up to the Royals to build some momentum by scoring.

Bobby led off the second with a lazy fly ball to center.  The centerfielder had a good break on the ball and caught it running in.  Terrace was up next, and he slashed a line drive down the left-field line that was a fair ball.  He turned and headed to second. The left fielder, Adriann Jones, was not known to have a strong or accurate arm, but this throw was right on the money, and Terrace was out.  Smart baseball does not always win games. When Terrance got to the dugout, that was what one of the coaches said to him.  Everyone in the park knew it was the right move for Terrace to go for a double, up against the arm of Jones.  But this time, it did not turn as expected.

Jackson was next up, and he hit a line drive into the left-field gap, ending up at 2B with a double.  The Royals had life.  Aaron singled, but the ball dropped directly in front of the centerfielder, and there was no way Jackson could score. There was now a man on first and third, and Cooper, the catcher, hitting 8th, hit a hard ground ball directly to the second baseman and was thrown out for the third out of the inning.

Art Holmes, once again, got through an inning without allowing a run.

The 9th hitter in the lineup, Tommy Thompson, led off after Cooper had ended the last inning. He took the count to 3 and 2 and then watched a curve break too low for ball four.

Now, it was up to Billy. The Chicago fans were rather quiet as they knew who Billy was, knowing full well, he could score Jackson from second base.

Billy took the first pitch for a ball. On the second pitch, he recognized the spin on a curveball. It was going to be inside, and he let it go by. "Ball Two," roared the Umpire. Billy was sure the next pitch was going to be a fastball. If it was even close, Billy was going to get good wood on it.

"Crack" was the sound the bat made when it connected with the ball. There were different kind of "cracks"; one you could tell it was a line drive, another you'd know it was a fly ball to an outfielder, but the "crack" off Billy's bat meant just one thing.....it was not going to come back into play. It sailed high over the center-field fence. Billy was not the type to stand and admire his HR, he bolted out of the box like he was hoping for a double, but he knew, like everyone else, he had a HR. The Royals had a 2-0 lead in a must game. They had to win this to even keep the series alive, and their hopes for another shot at the World Series. It felt good to have a two-run lead. Mack was up next and grounded to third. He hustled all the way, and the throw was low. To the naked eye, it looked like a tie, and everyone knew, "a tie goes to the runner." But, the naked eye isn't good enough in the majors. Mack was called safe, but the White Sox manager asked for a review by the people in New York.

Billy had a real hard time figuring out how the people in New York could make a better decision than the umps at the game. While waiting on the dugout steps, Billy asked Coach Kessler to explain it to him.

"Billy, the umpire in NYC who makes the final decision, has 12 camera angles to get the correct decision," explained Coach Kessler while he was looking at the angles the Royals were about to see it. They had five cameras, letting them see the play from five different angles, but it wasn't as good as the New York decision because that was final.

The umpires broke up, and the head umpire raised his hand and thumb into the night air, saying Mack was out. There was no arguing. It was the final decision. For the next three innings, the score remained 2-0 as Art was pitching a fantastic game. At the end of the 5th, the score remained 2-0, and Art had only given up two hits.

Billy had been up in the 4th but grounded out to 2B. The middle of the order was coming up. Arturo, Bobby, and Jackson. Any of them could hit a HR, but tonight, their bats were silent as all three hit grounders on the infield for outs.

In the bottom of the 6th, the first hitter lined a deep fly ball to Center, but Arturo got a jump on the ball at the crack of the bat, and made a diving, over his head catch. All of the Royals were tipping their hats at Arturo. The next batter hit a sharp grounder to the right of Billy. He dove for the ball and threw to first on his knees. Bobby stretched as far to his right as he could and somehow kept his foot on the base for out number two. This time, Art tipped his hat to Billy and Bobby as it took both of them making outstanding plays to get the White Sox runner. The next hitter popped up to Mack, and the game was going to the 7th inning, with the Royals still up 2-0.

The Royals didn't score, nor did the White Sox in the 7th inning. So now, going into the 8th inning, the score was still 2-0.

Billy was leading off in the top of the 8th. He knew if he could score, it would take some of the pressure off Art. He was already visualizing being on first and stealing second. On the second pitch, he hit a sharp line drive that fell directly in front of the right fielder. He was convinced that the ball was going to get by the right fielder, and he rounded first like he was going to second.....got halfway to second base and realized the right fielder picked it up clean and was throwing to second base. Billy realized he was not going to make it. He dug those metal spikes into the earth, stopped, and had to dive back to first. "Safe," indicated the umpire, and Billy breathed a sigh of relief. What if he'd been thrown out, and the Sox made a comeback. Billy was thankful for his metal spikes that dug into the earth like a bulldozer.

He was not given the sign to steal, and the inning produced no runs. It was now the bottom of the 8th, and the White Sox had been shut out by Art, and he had looked stronger each inning. The White Sox did not score, and neither did the Royals in the top of the 9th. Art was still pitching, and at this point, had only allowed three hits.

All the Royals knew they had to back Art up and keep the White Sox from scoring. If they did that, they'd get to play tomorrow night and be one game closer to the World Series.

Tablet Wilson was up first for the White Sox. On the first pitch, he hit a grounder almost directly over 2b. Mack couldn't reach it, but Billy did. He jumped in the air with a 180-degree twist and had the runner out by a step. Josh Hawkins was now hitting against Art. He hit a blast over Arturo's head in centerfield and ended up at 3b with a triple. Billy ran to the mound to calm Art down, who had hit his fist into his glove when he realized the ball was over Arturo's head.

Out walked Coach Kessler. Billy knew Cyde Brush would be coming in to try to get the last two outs and prevent Hawkins from scoring. The White Sox Manager called on Evan Tropple to pinch hit for Clowner. He hit left-handers, much better than righties, and he had power.

He fouled off ten straight pitches before finally, on the 12th pitch of his AB; he hit a line drive directly at Billy. He caught it by jumping as high as he could. One more out and Royals would still have a chance.

Jack Tomazie stood at the plate, hoping to knock Hawkins in. On the first pitch from Brush, Tomazie hit a drive to Billy's right. He backhanded it, set his feet, and threw a strike to Bobby at 1B. Three Outs! The Royals still had a chance.

# 22

## A Major Event

The Royals won the second game in Chicago.  Mack hit a soft line drive that fell in front of the centerfielder in the top of the 9th.  Billy had doubled and scored on Mack's hit, giving the Royals a three-run lead going into the last of the 9th.  Chicago didn't score.  The series was now tied 2-2 with the final game back in Kansas City.

On the flight back from Chicago, for some reason, Billy felt nervous. As the plane lifted off from the runway, it was apparent to all, something was wrong.  The aircraft circled out over Lake Michigan, but as Billy looked out the window, he could see that the plane was flying extremely low.  The captain's voice over the intercom could barely be heard because of the noise of the plane shaking.

"Everyone, we've got problems with the plane as we can not get it to climb high enough to get us above downtown Chicago.  We are going to try to get back to the airport, but everyone needs to make sure your seat belts are buckled."  He continued, "You need to lean forward in case we have to land the plane in Lake Michigan."  The plane continued to shake.  All of a sudden, Billy noticed flame coming from the engine on his side of the 737.  For the first time in a long time, he prayed, even outloud.  He wished he could remember that verse his Dad told him to read. He started saying the Lord's prayer outloud to himself, and, much to Billy's surprise,  several others began joining in. Before long, throughout the entire plane, players were praying, some saying the Lord's prayer with Billy, while others just buried their heads and prayed silently. Everyone knew the problems with the airplane were not minor.

The Captain came back on the intercom, "OK, everyone, tuck your head as low as you can and brace yourself. We are going to have to land the plane in the water. Your life belts are under your seat. Pull them out and hold on to yours." Less than a minute later, the plane hit the water. Water was rushing into the plane. Billy could see out the window, knowing that they were not underwater yet. He saw all the recovery boats around their airplane, but that didn't remove the fear as the plane began to sink. Billy was scared to death. He remembered a story his Dad told him, over and over, about his best friend, Don Doxee, who had died in a plane crash, although it was a test plane he was flying over the desert.

The captain's voice came over the intercom, but could barely be heard over all the screaming and praying. "There are recovery boats all around us, so before the plane sinks, we need to get each of you out of the plane. Your lifebelts will keep you afloat until a boat can pick you up. There are flashlights on each lifebelt that will come on automatically when you hit the water. We are opening the back door that goes to the cargo bay, where there is a slide that will get you off the plane before it goes underwater. The two flight attendants will lead you row by row to get to the slide. Make sure your life jackets are tightened. Once you hit the water, you will feel like you are freezing to death, but one of the recovery boats will reach you quickly. What you need to do is swim as far away from the plane as you can. When it goes under, there will be a zone around the plane that will take anything close by down with it. So swim as fast and far as you can."

Billy was surprised at how well the players followed the advice. No one rushed toward to back door and slide but instead came out row by row in a reasonably orderly fashion. Billy and Mack were on the third row from the front, and by the time they hit the water, most of the players were already off the plane. There were lights all around Billy, and he realized the lights were coming from each player's life jacket. He started swimming as fast as he could to get away from the plane. Even though Mack had gone out at the same time as Billy, it was dark, and he couldn't see his friend.

"Mack, where are you?" Billy yelled over all the commotion in the water. No answer. "Mack, where are you?" Again no answer. Billy hoped Mack was ahead of him, as he continued to swim as fast as he could to get away from the sinking plane. The life jacket intended to save lives made swimming much harder, but the boats recovering the players were staying as close to the wreckage as possible without taking the risk of going down with the plane.

It seemed like hours that Billy was in the cold water of Lake Michigan before someone picked him up. It was more like 10 minutes. The boat had several of the Royal players in it, but not Mack. The boat took off to get away from the airplane as fast as it could. Billy was still close enough to the plane to see the flight attendants and the captain slide down the chute, which meant there was no doubt, the airplane was going under. At least, everyone was off the plane.

It seemed there were thousands of people waiting on the beach for the boats to arrive, and once Billy's boat arrived, there were people there with blankets covering each of the players. As everyone waited to see if all the players and coaches had made it, people on the beach were building fire pits to keep the players from freezing to death after coming out of the cold waters. None were leaving the beach, although ambulances were waiting. They all wanted to make sure everyone had made it.

Billy kept looking for Mack. As cold he was, he left the fire pit built for him and two or three others. Billy had to find Mack. Bobby was in the fire pit area next to him, and he asked Bobby if he'd seen Mack.

"No, Billy, I haven't seen him," Bobby replied with fear in his voice the same as it had been in Billy's voice. He joined Billy in going to the different pits. There were seven fire pits, and the players huddled around each one. Billy and Bobby went to each fire pit but could not find Mack. After praying that Mack would be OK, Billy started yelling as loud as he could, but with all the other commotion, his voice could barely be heard. He found Coach Kessler and told him he could not find Mack, and they went down the chute together. After looking for Mack himself, Coach Kessler ran to a boat Captain, telling him that he believed one of the players was still in the water as he was not on the beach. The Captain started his boat immediately as Coach Kessler, Billy, and Bobby got on. Billy explained to the Captain that he and the missing player slid down the chute at the same time, but he was not on the beach. The blankets wrapped around them helped, but they were still freezing cold.

"Lord, let us find Mack and let him be OK," prayed Billy, outloud now.

There were wind gusts, causing waves on Lake Michigan, just like it was an ocean. The boat operator told Coach Kessler that if Mack was still in the water, he would have drifted far away from the airplane in the opposite direction of where most of the players had been picked up. He headed his boat far from where Billy thought they should go, but he was in charge and knew a lot more than Billy. Five minutes out in the water and no Mack. Another five minutes passed, and the boat operator said, "I think I see the life jacket light over to our left. Billy saw the light and watched closely as the boat circled the life jacket. It was floating by itself, and Mack was not in it.

The captain of the boat yelled, "don't worry......he will be close to the life jacket because the waves would have taken him this way." They all were shouting, "Mack, answer us." Billy thought he heard a faint voice. The Captain heard it as well and headed the boat the direction the sound. "Mack, are you there?" Billy and Bobby kept yelling. The Captain told them to be quiet so that he could hear the voice. The boat was closer because the faint sound became louder. It was Mack's voice, Billy could tell. It was pitch black on the water, now far away from the lights of Chicago. The Captain had a searchlight on the front of his boat, and he was aiming the light in the direction of Mack's voice.

Finally, Billy saw Mack treading water. The Captain took the boat right toward Mack, and as soon as he reached the area, he yelled out, "swim toward the boat." Mack did, and within minutes, he was in the boat, with everyone wrapping their blankets around him. It was evident to Billy that Mack was having serious problems. Billy hugged Mack, hoping his body temperature would help. Bobby hugged Mack from the opposite side. The Captain had the boat at full speed, heading back to the beach where the ambulances were waiting. As soon as the boat reached land, the Captain carried Mack to the Ambulance. Once Mack was in the ambulance, Billy realized how cold he was. "Are you as cold as I am," he asked Bobby. "No, I'm thinking about being on a beach in Panama," said Bobby, sarcastically. He was as cold as Billy. They looked for the fire pits and the rest of the team, but no one was there. So Billy and Bobby caught up with the ambulance and joined Coach Kessler and Mack at the last minute before the ambulance left. The driver told the Coach that the rest of the team had been taken to Northwestern Memorial Hospital, which was where he was taking us. There was a team of people waiting in the emergency ward to get heat back into Mack's body. Coach Kessler, Billy, and Bobby were cold as well, and the emergency team got them into rooms of their own with drips of something going into each of them. Billy asked his nurse about Mack.

"Son, your friend will be fine after we get his temperature up. He was lucky the water was so cold because cold water slows down the heartbeat as well as other body functions. He will recover just fine," the nurse explained.

Billy asked the nurse to call the parents of each of the three players to let them know they were all safe. The nurse got the numbers and called each, assuring the parents that their boys were all being treated and would be fine.

# 23

## Championship Series On Hold

The story of the Royals airplane going down was the biggest news of the night. Billy called his folks and Emma as soon as he could. Bobby called his parents too, but reporters at the hospital had already reported over CNN, Fox News, and most other networks that everyone aboard was safe. Because the hospital staff wanted to keep the players over-night and maybe longer, the final game of the series back at Kauffman Stadium had been postponed at least two days and possibly three, depending on how the players recovered. Billy was shocked at the mail, reaching the hospital the next day. People from all over the country, the world, were sending "get well" letters.

Most of the team was released the next morning, but Coach Kessler, Billy, Bobby, and Mack had to stay at the hospital for more tests. There was a Hyatt Regency close to the hospital, and the rest of the team went to the hotel to relax, waiting to see what the league would do about the remaining game in the American League Championship series. The TV news seemed to be about nothing except the Royals plane crashing into Lake Michigan. The players got to see all the rescue efforts. All except the coach, Billy, Bobby, and Mack because the doctors wanted to make sure they were okay. Billy just wanted out. But, the hospital staff kept doing more and more tests on the four of them, making them stay another day at the hospital.

The league got that information and announced the final game would not be for at least three more days.  The remaining team flew back to KC, where they had a short workout. But without the coach and most of the infielders, it was hard to get into the practice.

# <u>24</u>

## Baseball Again/Championship Game

The following day, the three were released from the hospital, with directions from the doctors telling them they should not play for at least three days. The league got the message from the hospital staff and rescheduled the final game for Saturday, giving the players two days to rest and then a day to work out before playing. The White Sox team had been in KC for four days now and were ready to play the final game. One thing the plane crash had done was to give all the starting pitchers plenty of time to rest.

The Royals knew they had to win this game to get to the World Series. All were just happy to be alive after the plane crash, but every player on the team from last year had one goal in mind, "get to the World Series and win it this year." To do that, they had to win this one game.

After a day of working out with the entire team, the coach decided to start Tommy Littlefield in the championship game. Usually, Coach Kessler would have gone with the starting pitcher in game one, but Tommy had finished the last two months of the regular season, winning five, losing none, and posting a 1.43 ERA over that time. Coach Kessler had confidence in Tommy.

The "K" was packed. It was standing room only, and Billy was sure it was the largest crowd he'd ever seen at the "K." They were cheering long before the game. After infield practice, the team headed toward their clubhouse, and Billy noticed most of the seats were already filled.  It was going to be an exciting game, and one the Royals had to win.  "With this crowd, how can we lose, " Billy thought to himself.

The team took the field for the National Anthem.  This time it was different than all other times he'd heard the National Anthem.  First, a minister prayed thanks that all of the team was here.  All the players on both sidelines placed their hats over their hearts as Nanette Wilson, a local girl, sang the National Anthem.  The grounds crew had pulled out a flag the size of the entire outfield, and each had a corner making it wave during the Anthem.  As Nanette sang her last note, fireworks exploded over the centerfield fence.  All Billy could think about was his prayer to God to find Mack.  He thought He must have heard me because, without the boat captain in charge, they never would have found Mack.  He wondered if the Captain of the boat was a Christian.  Billy had seen his folks, Mr. Booker and Emma, briefly.  They were thrilled to see him, but now, everyone was ready for game five of the American League series that would decide who would advance to the World Series.

Tommy was nervous during the first inning.  He walked the first batter, and the second laid down a perfect sacrifice bunt.  Now Tommy had the go-ahead run on second base with only one out.  The third hitter hit a hard line drive over second base, right where Billy was playing.  He dove for second base, hoping to get a double play.  "Yrrr Out," signaled the umpire.  There was a little arguing, but Billy was already in the dugout, getting his bat, But not the one he slept with all season.  That bat was in Lake Michigan.  The new bat felt almost the same.  He rubbed it up and down.   Bobby was convinced Billy was talking to his bat.  "Hey Billy, do you think talking to it is going to get you a hit?" Bobby quizzed his best friend.

"You never know, Bobby," Billy laughed.  He stepped into the "on deck" circle watching the warm-up pitches of "Slow Motion Morgan," as he was known around the league.  His nickname did not refer to his pitches, but how long he took between pitches.  He would pick up the rosin bag, run it around in his pitching hand, take his glove off, facing the outfield, and apparently talking to himself or the ball like Billy did his bat.  When he finally faced the batter, it took him a little while to put his foot on the rubber and look into his catcher for the sign.  This routine was followed with every pitch, so the Royals knew it would be a long game.  Billy wondered how long it would be before Donk came into the game…… Billy knew the Chicago White Sox manager would have started him, but if the White Sox could win this game, Donk would be available to start the first game of the World Series.

Billy decided to do the same thing to their pitcher, who had a good couple of months as a starter.  Billy got in the box.  Just as the pitcher stepped on the rubber, Billy stepped out of the box, knocking his bat against his metal spikes.  The pitcher could hear that sound…..different than the rubber spikes used mostly by the other players.  Billy stepped back into the box, while "Slo Mo" went through his regular routine.  When "Slo Mo" got on the rubber, finally, Billy stepped out again.  It was obvious this was a cat and mouse routine between the two players.

Neither wanted to give in to the other, but by the third time "Slow Mo" went through his routine, Billy stayed in the box and watched a high and outside pitch sail by. "Ball one," signaled the umpire. Billy knew his in and out of the batter's box had unsettled "Slow Mo," so Billy did it again, and sure enough, the next pitch was high and outside. "Ball Two," signaled the ump. Billy saw no reason to change his routine, so each time "Slow Mo" got to the rubber, Billy would step out and hit the bat against his metal spikes. On the third pitch, Billy watched the ball sail over his head. He now had a 3-0 count. Another ball and Billy would be ready to steal second. On this pitch, Billy got in the batter's box and stayed there until "Slo Mo" pitched. It was apparent that "Slow Mo" expected Billy to step out again, and when he didn't, "Slo Mo" threw another ball. Billy had not swung the bat but was on his way to first base. The crowd at the "K" was yelling as loud as Billy had ever heard.

On the first pitch to Mack, Billy had the steal sign. He knew that "Slo Mo" had a quick pickoff throw to first base, but he still took his 11-foot lead, thinking this pitcher is so upset, he will throw to the plate and not even try to pick him off. He was right as he slid into second base half a second before the ball arrived.

"Slo Mo" didn't even look at Billy on second. He was determined to get the next batter out. Billy took off running with plenty of time to spare because the catcher didn't bother to throw to third. By now, "Slo Mo" was visibly shaken. Mack decided to do the same thing he saw Billy do.....just as "Slo Mo" would put his foot on the rubber, Mack would step out, all the time Billy acting like he might try to steal home. "Slo Mo" was so upset; he threw a curve that bounced in front of the plate, and then toward the Royals dugout as their catcher had not been able to handle it. Billy was off running. He saw "Slo Mo" late in covering the plate, and Billy knew he was going to be safe, scoring the first run, without getting a hit, and Mack, the second hitter, still at the plate. The crowd was on their feet, shouting Billy's name.

Mack lined a single into left field but had to stop at first because Jack Daniels, the left fielder, picked the ball up and threw a strike to the second baseman. Auturo and Bobby both flied out, and Jackson hit a soft grounder back to the "Slo Mo," who threw him out.

The Royals led 1-0. Tommy settled down in the 2nd, 3rd, and 4th innings. He'd given up two harmless singles and was coasting along with his one run lead. Billy was up in the 3rd inning but hit a lazy grounder to the first baseman who had to dive to 1B to get him out, as Billy was giving it all he had and came close to beating it out for an infield single. Mack batting second showed no ill-effects from the plane crash, and he hit one that challenged Bobby for the longest HR of the season. The crack of the bat told the entire story. Kansas City fans were so in tune with the game of baseball; they could hear the sound of the ball meeting the bat and knew the Royals were going to lead by two runs. Mack got a standing ovation from the 42,000 fans that were fortunate enough to get tickets to Game Five.

In the 5th, Coach Kessler felt Tommy had gone as far as he should, and brought Butch Kelly in to pitch the middle innings. Like Tommy, he shut the

White Sox down for the next two innings, and the game was still 2-0, in favor of the Royals going into the top of the 7th inning.

Kelly walked the first batter he faced in the 7th, and Coach Wessler, the pitching coach, wasted no time in getting to the mound. He had Larry Thompson warmed in the bullpen. The coach talked to Kelly, instructing him to throw only curves to Little Jon and walked back to the dugout without motioning to bring in Thompson

Little Jon, the next hitter, was one of the hottest hitters in the month of July but had cooled off the last six weeks. Butch threw three curves, and each hit a corner of the plate for a strike. Little Jon looked at a called third strike. One out now.

Coach Kessler walked to the mound this time, motioning for each infielder to come to the mound. "Guys, in a 2-0 game, that decides who goes to the World Series, every pitch from here on is critical. Butch, you've been pitching fantastic, and I'm leaving you in to get the win. Guys, you know you are the best team in the American League, now is the time to prove it," said Coach Kessler, in a tone that built confidence.

Billy, listening intently to the coach, thought to himself that if he ever coached, he'd want to be like Coach Kessler. He made the players believe they were the best.

Bobby added an insurance run in the 8th inning, blasting one over the left-field fence that hit the Royals Hall of Fame building. It was now 3-0. Butch pitched the rest of the way, not allowing a run.

The Royals had won the American League Championship.

Not a single fan left the "K. Their hometown team was the American League Champions. The players were standing on the stage, accepting the trophy for winning the American League pennant. It was a joyful time. Billy was the recipient of the Most Valuable Player award. The Royals players were proud, and at the same time, excited about having the opportunity to win the World Series, finally.

The announcers were talking about the series just finished. "Game Seven and a 3-0 win. Is this what baseball is about or what! Billy Tankersly changed the game with his intelligence. He has baseball knowledge, far beyond his years. Get this, he hit .362, stole seven bases, and scored ten runs in the series. Considering the last game was a 3-0 game, his stats are amazing, " said the first announcer. The other announcer chimed in, "Did you see how he messed with the White Sox minds. He stepped in and out of the box against "Slo-Mo," and then the rest of the team followed Billy's example, and Slo-Mo was toast," he laughed.

The first announcer continued talking about the game they just announced. "This Bobby Bonds gives the Royals two potential All-Stars every year for years. They both are still only 20 years old. Did you know they grew up in the same block in Kansas City?"

He then ended the conversation about the game and started talking about the upcoming World Series. "This Royals team has a good chance of winning it all."

Due to the plane going down, the time between the last game of the American League championship and the start of the World Series was moved back two days.  Fortunately, the Kansas City Royals won more games than any other team, so they had the home-field advantage.  If the White Sox had won, the home field advantage would go to the Nationals who had the second-most wins.  The entire Nationals team was pulling for the White Sox.  When the Royals won, they won more than just the home field advantage; the Nationals were pulling for the White Sox so hard that now having to travel to Kansas City from DC was a significant factor in the upcoming series. They had pictured the wrong team winning the last game. The momentum had changed even before a single game of the World Series was played.

# <u>25</u>

## Time To Rest And Share His Faith

Billy spent the night at home, even though the rest of the team was at the Hyatt. He had never fully recovered from the plane crash and looking for Mack. He felt as though that fear would stay with him for the rest of his life and, to this day, believes God saved them all, including Mack. He wanted to stay home to talk to his folks and Emma about the plane crash, and something that happened while the plane was going down.

"Dad, do you remember what happened at a game in Emporia?" asked Billy.

"Well, son, I don't remember the game at all. What I remember is the hospital," answered his Dad with a smile.

"Do you know what you told me to do that night?" Billy asked.

"Sure I do....I told you to pray," replied Mr. Tankersly.

"Well, as the plane was going down, I was scared to death, as was everyone. I started praying and then saying the Lord's prayer outloud," said his son. "Everything happened so fast, I didn't realize it at the time, but every player on the team joined me in saying the Lord's Prayer."

"Then, when I couldn't find Mack, I knew he was someplace out there in the darkness of the night, so I prayed again ....this time, that we would find Mack, which seemed impossible because it was pitch black that night; even the moon had gone down," Billy shared with his Dad, Mom, and Emma.

"When we saw his life jacket with no one in it, I thought he'd drowned, but once again, I prayed and believed at that very moment we were going to find Mack. Just then, the Captain of the boat said, "be quiet, I think I hear something." "Coach Kessler and I could probably hear each other breathing; it was so quiet," said Billy. "You can't imagine how dark and quiet it is at night way out in Lake Michigan," he continued. "But when we all quit talking, we could hear a faint, "help me" coming from our right," Billy's voice got soft as he was telling them how it felt finding Mack. The Captain turned the boat that way, and Mack's voice got louder and louder, and suddenly, the captain's searchlight spotted him.

"Never in my wildest dreams could I have imagined what took place that night," said Billy. "I believe if I hadn't been praying, we would not have found Mack, but it wasn't just me praying," Billy explained. "I had long talks with Mack about the Lord and praying, and the next day, he told me if it hadn't been for his praying, he would have given up out there in the darkness.

Emma spoke up, "Billy, you've never talked to me about the power of prayer."

"It just hasn't been at the forefront of my mind when we have been together....heck, my mind has been on you," Billy confessed. "Now, after seeing what happened, I don't think there will ever be a day where I don't  put the Lord first."

"Billy, since you've never really brought up the Lord in our conversations, at least not to this level, I didn't share my beliefs with you," Emma said.  I do believe in Jesus, just not in a personal way like you've described.

"Em, I read the Bible every night before going to bed. I am constantly amazed by the strength of God's Word. It's sort of funny, but Babe Ruth and Ricky Henderson had always been my hero's....and Dad, of course. But after spending time in the Book of John, I found a new hero...yep, even greater than Ricky, and even Dad," Billy smiled.

Mr. Tankersly was sitting across the room from Billy, as was his Mom. He could see tears in both of their eyes. "Billy, we had no idea you had this relationship with Jesus," spoke his Mom. "We've prayed every night since you were born for you to find Jesus, but we left it in your hands. We've never been church-going people, but we read the Bible and pray together each night. We did go to church after you were born, but the preacher talked about things we'd already studied. Mom and I talked about it, thinking if we did not go to church, how were you going to find the Lord. We did not want to force you away from God because you were pretty strong-willed as a young boy, and you didn't like anyone to tell you what to do....so we didn't, but we continued to pray every night for you," stated his Mom.

"Wow, I didn't know any of this. The only time you've ever even mentioned the Lord or praying was at the Emporia game....or rather, the hospital, when Dad told me to pray, and it would all work out. I didn't even know how to pray, but that night, I had a personal talk with the Lord. And I swear, I heard an answer back saying, "Billy, you are going to be fine." I thought it was just me saying that to myself, but the more I read the Bible, I know it was the Holy

Spirit," Billy said with emotion Emma had never seen from him.

"And right now, the Holy Spirit is telling me to get to bed to get some sleep before the World Series excitement that will keep me awake every night, "Billy smiled. He hugged everyone, grabbed his bat, and headed to his bedroom, leaving Emma and Billy's folks alone to digest what Billy had just shared with them. The next morning, he laughed for maybe the first time since the plane crash when his Dad said, "OK, youngster....this is your series....go win it." Billy laughed and said, "Is there any doubt about us winning the World Series?"

He didn't want to ride to the stadium with all of them because he wanted his mind to be 100% on the game, so he called an Uber. As he got in the car, he kissed Emma goodbye saying, "I'll see you after we win the first two games before we have to fly to Washington, DC. He felt better than any day since the plane crash.

# <u>26</u>

## Dreams Do Come True

When Billy walked into the clubhouse, Bobby came up, hugged him, and said, "do you remember when we were on the Yankees Little League team, and you told me, someday, we will be playing for the Royals in a World Series." Billy smiled, saying, "Bobby, you may have the best memory of anyone I've ever known....one time, I said that."

"Well, I never forgot it, even when I was in Austin and you were still in KC, I dreamed of us playing together again, and winning a World Series," Bobby told his best friend.

"OK best buddy, let's go out there and bring the championship home to KC," Billy laughed. Bobby could feel that Billy was well-prepared mentally to win the series.

As the teams came out of the clubhouse, you could tell this was far different than any other game he'd ever played in. There were flags all over the park, and each player was introduced as they stood on the baseline closest to their dugout. The announcer introduced the Nationals first, with Pepper Grapper getting the most applause. Everyone knew he'd had a great year, leading the entire National League in on-base percentage, hitting average, and HRs.

Then it was time to introduce the KC Royals to their home fans. First, all the players that were not starting, and then the starting team. Because Billy was leading off, he was called first. "Ladies and

Gentlemen, our home-grown Billy Tankersly" The crowd was cheering for him so loud that he had cold chills. When Bobby was introduced, the announcer referred to him as "home-grown," and the crowd roared again. Once all the players had been announced, and an American Flag covering the entire outfield had been spread out, Peggy Snodgrass, another local star, sang the National Anthem. And then the announcer blared out, "Play Ball."

Coach Kessler decided to start Butch Kelly in the opener. It was the right decision as he struck out three straight batters, including Pepper Grapper. There was a constant roar from the fans, but when Kelly struck out Grapper, it seemed like an earthquake, there was so much noise. The vibration could be felt all over the field.

This was Billy's dream, as he had watched many Royals games over the years, thinking at each game, "someday, I'm going to be playing for the Royals, and we will win the World Series." Starting at SS and hitting lead-off was an added twist to Billy's dream.

When the announcer said, "Leading off for the Royals, playing shortstop, Billy Tankersly," the crowd went wild. Just as he'd done in Lexington in his first professional game, he stood at the plate, looking all around, making sure this was a memory he'd never forget. Finally, he stepped in the batter's box, remembering what Bobby had said about this being their dream since Little League.

On the mound for the Nationals was Grant Bubble, a pitcher who won the Cy Young award last year for being the best pitcher in the National League.

Determined to get a hit, Billy realized he was nervous and decided to let the first pitch go by to settle down. "Strike One," yelled the ump. He had to shout to be heard by the pitcher because of the noise in the stadium. Bubble had thrown him a fastball on the first pitch. Would he throw another fastball after Billy let that one go by without swinging?

Billy felt confident that Bubble would throw another fastball. He guessed wrong as Bubble threw him a curve that made Billy look silly swinging at it, as it almost hit the plate. "Stike Two," yelled the ump. Billy stepped out of the box, hit his metal spikes with his bat...and just like the crack of the bat on a HR, the sound of those metal spikes could be heard over the noise of the crowd. He watched the next three pitches go by for balls, so the count was now full, 3 & 2.

This time, Billy guessed right, and as he saw the spin on the ball, he knew it was a curve. He blasted a line drive down the right field line. It was hit so hard that it bounced off the wall right into the right fielder's glove. Because the play was right in front of Billy, he knew it was a single, and there was no point in trying to stretch it into a double.

As it had been all year, Mack was hitting second. He and Billy made the best double play combo in the American League, but also two of the best hitters on the team, along with Bobby. They worked well together as Mack, for the most part, could sense when Billy was going to steal second. He'd been fooled in the White Sox series when Billy didn't steal on the first pitch, and Mack hit into a Double Play on the next pitch. This time, Mack had decided not to swing the bat until either Billy had stolen second base, or he had two strikes on him. It didn't take long before Billy was on second base with his first stolen base in the World Series. Bubble hadn't even pitched to Mack, so now with Billy on second, all Mack had to do was get a hit to drive his best friend in.

Finally, Mack got to see Bubble's fastball, but it was so far inside that it almost hit Mack. It was apparent; Billy was already distracting this former Cy Young winner. Billy had played enough this year and studied opposing pitchers that he knew Bubble was upset that Billy was on second base. He threw another ball to Mack. It was a curve that no way Mack could hit it as it was almost a foot over his head. This was not what a curveball was supposed to do.....it should have broken down. Billy knew Bubble had no choice but to throw Mack a strike. He took his normal lead and broke for third the second his arm was in a throwing motion to the plate. Mack fouled it off, so Billy had to go back to second, and now Bubble was paying more attention to the fleet-footed, metal spikes guy, Billy Tankersly. Bubble had heard all about Billy's speed but had no idea just how fast this kid was. The National's best pitcher was rattled. He threw two more balls to Mack, both outside, and Mack walked. He was now on first base with Arturo coming up. Mack knew that Billy might steal on any pitch, so it was Mack's job to watch Billy so he could break for second the moment Billy broke for third. They had many double steals this year, and Mack was ready for Billy to break for third.

It happened on the first pitch to Arturo. Billy knew by now, Bubble had to throw a strike to the next batter after walking Mack. Bubble looked back to second two times; he finally lifted his leg to where it crossed the rubber, and Billy and Mack were running.

The throw to third was close, but Billy slid by the base, grabbing it with his hand.  He was safe.  Now with runners on second and third, Bubble was in trouble. He had to throw a strike to Arturo because he knew about Bobby's power, who was up right after Arturo.  Sure enough, it was a meatball directly over the center of the plate.  Arturo lashed a line drive in the gap between the left fielder and centerfielder. Billy and Mack scored easily, giving the Royals a two-run lead, and only three batters had faced Bubble.  Bobby gave Billy and Mack fist bumps as they headed to the dugout, and he headed toward the batter's box.

Bobby was as excited to be playing in a World Series game as Billy.  Their dream had come true. Now, they had to score more runs to give Butch a cushion.  Bobby didn't waste any time. He knew Bubble would throw him a hittable pitch, and he hit it.....so far over the left-field fence, it hit the "Royals Hall of Fame" building in left-field above the seats. Two more runs as Arturo and Bobby scored, making it a 4-0 lead in the first inning, with Bubble only facing four Royals hitters.  The crowd was in 7th heaven, seeing their Royals jump off to a big lead in the first inning....and they were loud.

Josh Martin, the pitching coach for the Nationals, strolled to the mound.  There was no one warming up in the bullpen, so this was a meeting to calm Bubble down.

Terrace, waiting for the meeting to be over, stepped into the batter's box.  He was anxious to hit against Bubble before the Nationals pulled him. Bubble threw him three straight fastballs, and on the third one, Terrace hit a line drive single over the SS's head.  Five batters had faced the former Cy Young winner, and all had reached base.  Jackson was ready to add to the Royals lead.  On the first pitch, he hit a ground ball between the SS and 3B.....the third baseman reached it, threw to second for the force out, and the second baseman jumped to avoid Terrace sliding into second base, and still had enough on his throw to get Jackson out.  With two outs, Aaron came up ready to start another rally.  But Bubble was gaining some confidence after the double play, and he struck Aaron out on three pitches.

The score remained 4-0 until the 6th inning when Pepper Grapper led off with a long HR over the centerfield fence.  Kauffman Stadium had the largest playing surface of any major league park, and the center field fence was 410 feet from home plate.  Pepper had found the sweet part of his bat to hit one that far.  Coach Kessler knew if Pepper got that much wood on his bat, it was time to bring in a reliever.  He walked to the mound, neither quickly or slowly.  He talked to Butch for probably 20 seconds, and the ump came out to break up the party as the entire infielders were standing close to the mound to see what Coach Kessler was going to do.  Just then, the coach waved his left arm, signaling the bullpen that he wanted Farmer Hart to take over.  Farmer had been in the minors most of the year, but about a month ago, he was promoted after winning 13 games for the Storm Chasers.  He had been a starter for Omaha, but Coach Kessler had been using Farmer as a reliever.

Farmer had a wicked curveball that looked like it was going to hit a left-handed batter and then curved over the plate for a strike.  Two more pitches just like that, and he had his first World Series strikeout. The next batter was a right-handed batter, where Farmer's curve would appear to be outside, and then wrap around the corner of the plate to be a strike. But, he never got to face the right-handed batter.

Coach Kessler walked to the mound again, and this time on his walk, he waved his right arm up, meaning that Maverick Pemper was being called in. Maverick threw fastballs as his main pitch. He hit 100 mph on most pitches, except his changeup, which only reached 78 mph. It took Maverick eight pitches to get out of the inning.

In the last of the 7th inning, Billy got up for the third time. After hitting a grounder to 2nd base in his second time up, Billy was determined to get on base to steal another one.

It took one pitch, and Billy hit a line drive over the second baseman who had been playing in shallow right field. Billy was limited to a single as the right fielder was not far behind the second baseman. He picked it up and threw to the SS, covering 2B keeping Billy at 1B.

Mack adopted the same game plan he had in the first...." Do not swing until Billy is on 2nd, or I have two strikes on me," he thought. On the first pitch, Billy made Mack's job a lot easier by stealing second and being safe by a 'country mile.' That freed Mack up to hit the first good pitch he saw, not having to wait for Billy to steal.

None of the 48,000 people jammed into Kauffman Stadium were surprised at what happened next. Mack took a slider inside, and before he could even look up to regain his composer after almost being hit, Billy had stolen third base. With the score being 4-1, another run would be an insurance run against the Nationals hitting a grand slam, and with Pepper coming up in the top of the 8th, it was possible for the Nationals to score a lot in a hurry. If Billy could score, it would take a grand slam to even tie the game. All of this was going through Billy's mind, realizing that one more run would put the game almost out of reach. He was on his toes, ready to steal home if a pitch got away from the catcher. Mack didn't see a pitch even close, so the Royals had men on first and third. Arturo hit a slow ground ball to the SS, who had to decide on going for the double play or trying to get Billy at the plate. He threw to the plate. It was the wrong decision as Billy slid in with the 5th run for the Royals. Now the Royals had men on first and second with Bobby coming up.

The Nationals manager walked briskly to the mound waving his left arm in the air, calling for Steve Clark, usually their closer. It was a good move as Bobby hit a hard grounder to the second baseman who threw to the SS, and he relayed a perfect throw to first for the double play. But Coach Kessler wanted one more run, so he brought Art Damon off the bench to pinch-hit for Terrance. Art did exactly what Coach Kessler had wanted. He singled to center bringing in Mack and giving the Royals a 6-1 lead.

Billy didn't get up again, but the Royals won the game, 6-1, and now had a one-game lead over the Nationals. In the American League championship, they only played five games to determine the champions, but in the World Series, it was a seven-game series. Winning the first game was always important.

Coach Kessler called the team together in the clubhouse, warning everyone that the team still had to win three more. "Don't get too cocky, guys, but what a great game this was. Congratulations. Get a good night's sleep as we've got to do it all over again tomorrow night," concluded the Coach's advice.

Billy's Dad and Mom, plus Mr. Booker and Emma, were all waiting for him when he came out of the clubhouse. "Great game," said Mr. Booker first. Then his Dad and Mom chimed in with more praise. Finally, Emma said, "You grounded to 2B your second time up....how are you going to beat Ricky's record doing that?" she smiled. Billy took her in his arms, telling her to quit paying so much attention to baseball because she had school work to get done. She laughed and told him, "This is Saturday. Billy. I don't have classes on Saturday." They both laughed.

# 27

## A Special Night

Billy told them that the Coach had asked all the players to stay at the hotel. Since Billy was the only player who lived in KC and had his own bed to sleep in, he couldn't figure out why the Coach wanted to have him stay in the hotel. But he hugged his fan base, telling them he'd see them tomorrow, and "Please yell louder." They all laughed as Billy boarded the team bus to go to their hotel.

He sat next to Bobby on the bus. These two young men, who had grown up together since they were eight years old, knew what the other was thinking before it was even said. They were 'best friends.'

"Hey, Billy, you've been playing well. It's been fun watching you, and I think everyone on the team is learning smart baseball from the example you've set. I'm proud to be your best friend," Bobby said with a funny laugh. Billy said, "Thanks, best friend, you've had a good year, too. Can you believe we were playing ball in Donna's yard because she had a fence and room to play hardball? Wow, we must have been really small then because it was hard to hit it over the fence," Billy laughed.

"How many steals do you have this year, Billy?" Bobby asked. "My goal was to reach 100 in my first full year in the majors because Ricky did it. But I ended up with 89. I hate to say it, but I let the pressure get to me. I was thrown out three times in the last ten games," Billy answered with the way he viewed those last ten games. "I've passed the 100 mark counting the playoffs and World Series, but it's not the same as Ricky doing it in the regular season," Billy added.

"It's sort of funny you had to ask. Heck, I know you hit 48 HR's, drove in 112, and had five stolen bases on your own," Billy kidded his best bud. "You are going to be chosen as Rookie of the Year."

Bobby responded immediately, "Are you dense, Mr. Tankersly? You've won it hands down."

Both young men laughed, realizing two kids that started playing baseball together on the streets of Kansas City when they were eight years old were now both up for Rookie of the Year. "That's pretty amazing, Billy," Bobby said.

"Now we have to win a World Series," Billy brought them back to reality. "We have a one-game lead and need to win the next game because then we go to Washington, DC, for three games unless we win the next three games. Who do you imagine Coach will start pitching tomorrow?" he asked Bobby.

"It has to be Tim Wood," Bobby replied. "I heard the Coach talking to someone earlier today before the game even started. He mentioned, if we won, he'd throw Tim and Jack Murawski in the next two games."

Just then, the bus arrived at the hotel. The team ate together in a  private room in the restaurant, but as they entered, they saw something funny. There were name tags in front of each seat. The Coach was having them sit in a strange order. All the team wondered, what was going on because he'd never done this before, not once all year.

It seemed like years before he entered. No waitress had shown up, which was also strange. The room was deathly quiet.

You could hear Coach's shoes hitting on the floor as he walked to the head of the table. He sat down, pulled his chair up, and looked up and down both rows of players, without saying a word.

Finally, he spoke, "Men, I have you here in a certain order because, even though some of you speak a language different than English, you've done your best to speak English, and I've admired you for that. Now what I'd like is for the player on your right to teach you ten words in his language," the Coach commanded.

All the guys sort of relaxed in their chairs in relief that it was a fun thing and not something serious. Billy sat next to Aintza Martinez. "OK, Aintza, teach me ten words," he said to the utility infielder who had backed up Mack in probably 20 games during the regular season.

"Aintza, the meaning of that word means I'm a comedian," Aintza laughed. "So here are ten words we speak in the Dominic. "Guey, Agus, Chingon, Fresa, Mande, Andale, Carnal, Pinche, Chingar, Blanco," Aintza laughed. "Guess what they mean, Billy?" Aintza said in broken English.

"Hmmm," Billy thought. "OK, Agus is a meat, right?" he asked. Aintza was going to be laughing for hours with these words and playing a guessing game with Billy. "No, Billy, Agus means 'look out!' OK, let's forget the guessing game because you are not going to be close on any of these words. To me, they are natural, but to you, well......" Aintza smiled.

"Let me tell you the meaning of each, and then tomorrow you can tell me if you remember them. Guey means friend. Chingon is the cool way of saying Awesome. Fresa is a strawberry. Mande mean, say that again, I didn't hear you. Andale means hurry up. Carnal is what you and Bobby are. Best Friends. Pinche means damn. You've got to be angry in my country to use that word. Chingar.....gezzzz, there is no way to explain that in the English language. I don't even know where to begin. OK, the last word, you are Blanco, Billy. It means white," Aintza laughed. Billy laughed too, but his focus was trying to remember the words. "Let me see how many I can remember, Aintza," Billy started. Agus is not meat. It means....doggone it.....it means look out. Guey means guy or friend. Chingon means....I don't know. Fresa is a strawberry. Ahhhh, give me a hint....oh, Pinche means a swear word, like Damn. Carnal....is that right, Carnal?" Aineza shook his head, yes. "Carnal means....I forget," Billy gave up. Aintza said, "you did good, Billy. Carnal means best friends. The only other words you didn't remember were Chingar, Andale, and Mande. Do you remember what Mande means? It means say that again, I didn't hear you. Andale. Do you remember what that means?" he asked Billy. "I think it means something like hurry up," Billy responded. "Perfect," Aintza said. "And to be honest, I have no idea what the word chingar means. It's used in so many different ways; there is no way to explain it."

"I live in the Dominican Republic. It is an island with Haiti on one end on Dominican on the other. We play baseball from the time we are kids. I'd love to have you come over and visit my family during the off-season," Aintza offered. Then he added, "now that you speak Spanish."

Just then, the coach spoke. "Fellows, I hope you've learned something. We've gone an entire season, and you guys who don't speak English naturally have done a tremendous job in doing your best. For you on the team who speak English naturally, I hope you learned something this evening. I know you are wondering, why now after winning the first game of the World Series? I've been thinking about it for weeks, and I am sorry it's now, but I was not going to let another day pass without doing it. I want you English speaking Americans to appreciate how hard your fellow team-mates have worked without you even realizing it. They've had two games every day, one playing baseball and the other wondering what in the world you were talking about," the coach explained, with a smile. "OK, let's eat."

After dinner, it was Aintza, who Billy hung out with, in the lounge. Aintza was old enough to drink alcohol, but he ordered a coke with Billy. Aintza was amazed that Billy knew he'd hit .236 and had two homers. "Thank you, Billy, for hanging out with me. I am so honored that you know my batting average," Aintza said. "That is amazing. Do you know the batting averages of everyone on the team?" Aintza asked. "No, not everyone, but I took a liking to how you played the game. You always hustle, and I've admired that. So, I started checking out stats for others, in addition to you, but "the comedian" was someone I've been really interested in," Billy smiled.

Aintza went to bed that night feeling very much appreciated. Had it not been for the Coach doing his surprise "learn another language" before dinner, he never would have known that Billy was "carnal."

# 28

## Game Two Extra Innings

Game two of the World Series turned out to be the most exciting game of the season. The fans got their money's worth as it was now the bottom of the 19th inning, in a 4-4 tie.

Billy was first up. "Funny how things come into your mind," he thought as he stepped into the batter's box. "I need to be watching the spin on his ball. I feel confident that he is going to throw a curve on the first pitch."

Sure enough, it was a hard breaking curve where the bottom just dropped out. Even though Billy was expecting a curve, he was shocked at how much the ball dropped. He swung and missed it by quite a bit. Billy stepped out of the box, hit the bat against his metal spikes. It seemed all during the season when he did this; he was relaxed on the next pitch. The Nationals pitcher was the 6th Nats pitcher. Billy wondered if the series did go seven games; would they even have a pitcher left? However, this guy, Grady Beneniz, had been a closer for the Nationals all year until the last two weeks when he got hit by a line drive in the National League playoffs. The ball left the bat at 109 mph. He fell to the ground and was taken out immediately. He pitched one more game after that in the National League series but did not get in the first game of the World Series. Billy figured Beneniz might be reluctant to throw a fastball and have it come back at him that fast, so the young SS was waiting for another curve. He guessed right and decided to go the opposite way, hitting to left field instead of the way they had him played with the switch on the right side of the infield. The pitch was on the inside. He let it go by for a ball.

As Billy looked over the field, he saw the SS now playing close to second base, with no one covering third base. It was time for a bunt if he got the right pitch. It was another curve; only it didn't break as much. Billy started running as he laid a perfect drag bunt down the third baseline. The third baseman was now on the 1B side of second base, with only the SS covering the left side. For some reason, he was expecting Billy to bunt, and as soon as Billy indicated a bunt, the SS was running toward third. He picked the ball up barehanded and threw off-balance to 1B, hoping to get Tankersly out. The throw ended up in short right field as the ball hit the first baseman's glove and darted off toward the grandstands. Billy didn't miss a beat. He rounded first, knowing that he had second base. But as he neared the bag, he looked at his third base coach, who was signaling to come on to third. Billy had no idea where the ball was, just that the coach was waving him to third. He wondered if the ball had skipped into right field. But as he approached third base, the coach was waving him on. "What?" Billy thought. "It was a bunt."

He followed his coach's signals and headed for the plate. What Billy didn't know was that the first baseman had picked the ball up by the grandstands, turned to threw to second base. But the throw was off the base where no one could reach it, and the ball rolled into short centerfield where again, no one could get to it by the time Billy was almost to third. When Coach signaled Billy to keep running, he pounded those metal spikes into the dirt and ran as fast as he could.  He saw the catcher getting ready for a throw. Billy knew he would have to slide on the outside of the plate and touch home plate with his outstretched fingers as he slid past it.  He had no idea if he was safe or out.

The 47,000 people at the K were on their feet, and even though Billy couldn't hear or see what the umpire had called, he knew from the crowd noise he'd been called safe, and the Royals had won the second game of the series.

The Royals announcers were almost silent. They couldn't believe what they'd seen with their own eyes.  John Benson, the Royals announcer for the past 15 years, was beside himself. "Did you see what I just saw?" he asked his color commenter, Ty Hill, in a shrill voice. "I've never seen anything like that. Billy Tankersly has to be the fastest runner ever to play the game unless it was Ricky Henderson," he added.

"For crying out loud, he bunted!" Benson yelled into the microphone.  "And the Royals win with a bunt single that turned into a game-ending error, maybe two to let him score, in the bottom of the 19th. Unbelievable," he continued to talk in a voice much louder than usual.  Part of that was that the crowd, all 47,000 were in their seats, yelling, "Billy, Billy, Billy."

By now, the on the field announcers had a microphone in front of him with the camera's rolling. "Billy, what made you think you could score as the ball was in short centerfield?" Rex Trombone, the on-field announcer, asked.  "I had no idea where the ball was, I just followed the coaches signals and rounded third with a full head of steam behind me. But, I will admit....if I'd had to run one more base, I think I would have dropped. I was completely worn out, just like every other player out there after 19 innings," Billy admitted. "Well, Billy, that was probably the most exciting finish to a game I've ever seen, " spoke up Rex. The crowd that normally shouted, "Let's go Royals, Let's go Royals" was now still shouting, "Billy, Billy, Billy."

As the team filed into the clubhouse, it seemed every player gave Billy a big hug, or a slap on the back, congratulating him on almost winning the game by himself. He knew better than that in a 19 inning game but was as happy ...and drained....as he had ever been after a game. He still couldn't believe he'd scored on his drag bunt to the left side of the field.

After the game, Billy joined his folks, Mr. Booker and Emma. All were as excited as everyone else in the stands and dugout. Mr. Booker was the first to say anything, "Billy, I am so proud of you....not just for scoring the winning run, or the way you accomplished it, but the fact you made this old man feel mighty happy about all the days we'd practiced together, by showing your speed tonight." Billy hugged Mr. Booker, telling him how much he appreciated all the days he worked with him to make him the hero of Game Two as fast as he was. "I think maybe this is the first game a Hall of Fame Groundskeeper has won a world series game," Billy laughed, although he was so hoarse from cheering his team on for five hours, it was hard for him even to talk now.

His Dad hugged him, saying, "Billy, you amaze me all the time, but this was unreal. You scored the winning run on a bunt single," his Dad laughed. Billy thought he saw tears in his mom's eyes, and Emma's. He hugged them both, thanking them for helping him. Neither said a word to Billy, at least in his memory back at the hotel, packing up for the flight to Washington DC to play the third game in the Nationals Park.

On the flight to the Nation's capital, Billy and everyone else was sound asleep the entire flight. They were exhausted. The only person with his eyes open was Coach Kessler, figuring out who to pitch in the third game. He thought he had it figured out, but now….he just wasn't sure. That one problem was on his mind the entire flight.

# <u>29</u>

## Washington, DC

Billy had no idea who Coach Kessler was going to start in the third game, but he hoped it would be Jim Horstman, who he'd played with at Omaha for almost a full year, and who he'd become friends with, in the minors. Now the two boys were in the World Series together.

As game-time approached, Coach Kessler told Jim and all the other players, that he would be starting tonight. Coach Kessler had a theory that if you wait until almost game time before announcing the starting pitcher, it takes the pressure off him of having to think about it for a day or so.

The Washington Nationals ballpark had a seating cap of 47,000, closely resembling the "K." The Nationals knew they badly needed to win the first game in DC. Since the Royals were the visiting team, Billy was first up. After working to a 3 & 2 count, he hit a lazy grounder to the 2nd baseman who was playing in short right field. As hard as Billy ran, he was thrown out with a great play from Tommy Garcia, the Nationals second baseman. Mack didn't fare any better as he hit a grounder to the shortstop, Andy Long. He was thrown out by two steps. Arturo stuck out on four pitches, and the Nationals were facing Jim Horstman for the first time. Most had not seen him pitch since he was in the minors until the September call up.

Jim didn't let the Royals down. He struck the side out, including Pepper Grapper. Billy didn't get up again until the 4th inning as both pitchers were in a World Series duel, with neither pitcher allowing a hit through three innings.

Billy had watched their pitcher, Josh Hawkings, like a hawk. He saw Hawkings start each batter off with a fastball. His control had been almost perfect. He was hitting first the inside corner and then the outside corner, hitting the black part of the home plate on almost every pitch. So far, Billy had not seen a weakness in Hawkings. When he stepped into the box to face the Nationals all-star pitcher, he realized the catcher was setting up on the side of the plate where the pitch was going to be thrown.

As Hawkings started his windup, Billy glanced behind him. He saw the catcher on the outside of the plate. Sure enough, it was a fastball on the outside corner of the plate. "Strike One" signaled the umpire as Billy stepped out of the box to tie his shoe. He was going to try anything to get Hawkings a little upset. After tying the first shoe, Billy purposely tied the other shoe as well, making Hawkings wait just a little longer. As Hawkings started his windup, Billy called time. The umpire called time before Hawkings could throw the ball. The young shortstop had already been at bat for two minutes, and Hawkings had only thrown one pitch.

Billy stepped back in the box, ready to swing, but the ball was outside by two inches. With the count at 1-1, Hawkings threw another fastball on the inside of the plate. Billy was ready. He swung and missed. Now the National's pitcher had the count in his favor.

Billy had noticed that when Hawking's got ahead of a batter, he would throw a curve. He watched the ball from the time it left the pitchers hand. The pitch didn't seem to have much of a rotation, so Billy knew it was a fastball again. He watched the pitch cross the plate on the outside corner and knew it was a strike. Rather than argue with the umpire, Billy turned and slowly walked back to the dugout. All the players wanted to know what Hawkings had thrown to strike Billy out. "It was a fastball on the outside corner of the plate" Billy told them. Then he added, "I was pretty sure he was going to throw a curve, and the fastball went by me with my bat on my shoulder because I'd guessed wrong. I don't think we can guess against this guy," added Billy.

Mack was able to at least get his bat to touch the ball, but it was a popup. Arturo struck out for the second time in the game.

Going into the bottom of the 4th, both pitchers had no hitter's going. The crowd in the Nationals park knew this was a game where one run could win it.

Jim also had a no-hitter going, and after striking out the first two hitters in the 4th, he had to face Peter Grapper. During the season, Grapper hit .327, but in the playoffs, he was hitting .420, so the crowd expected him to get on. He not only got on, but he also hit a line drive that was about 20 feet over the centerfield fence. Billy thought to himself, "that ball would have just been a long fly ball in the Kansas City park." Unfortunately, they were not playing at the "K." As Peter rounded second base, he smiled at Billy and said something to him. To Billy, it sounded like he said, "quite a game," and Billy replied, "Nice hit, Peter." If it had been a regular-season game, the hitter and Billy would send jives to each other, but here in the World Series, there was an acknowledgment by both players that this was what a World Series game should feel like. The next batter hit a ground ball to Billy, who picked it up flawlessly and threw a strike to Bobby at first for the final out in the 4th inning. The score was now 1-0 with the Nationals leading.

Grapper's HR won the game for the Nationals as the Royals were shut out. Billy was 0-3 with one walk and one stolen base.

The clubhouse was pretty quiet. The team was hoping and expecting to come to DC and win the World Series there. Now with two games left in the nation's capital, it would be possible for the Nationals to take the series lead. The Royals had to win one of the next two games, or they would be going back to KC trailing the Nationals.

The following night, the Royals bats went silent again, only getting two hits, one by Billy and one by Bobby. They lost 6-1, and now the series was even.

Every Royals player knew they had to win the next game. You could feel the pressure in the clubhouse. Someone had to change the attitude, or they would lose the next game for sure.

Billy spoke up. "Guys, let's just have fun tomorrow. When we are relaxed, having fun, no one can beat us." The clubhouse livened up after Billy's two-sentence pep talk. Back at the hotel, the team had their late-night dinner and hit the sack.

Morning came too early for Billy, even though it was 10:00 AM. The team was to be at the National's stadium by 1:00 to loosen up, take infield, and hitting practice. They were allowed to be on the field for two hours with the Nationals following the Royals. It was a good workout as everyone seemed to be up to the challenge of winning tonight's game, sending the series back to Kansas City with a one game lead.

Coach Kessler came in to announce who he was starting in the fifth game. "Guys, listen up. I've decided to start Tommy Levin tonight. Tommy, I know you are a reliever, but you've been extremely reliable for two good innings. If we get two clean innings out of you tonight, we can bring in Butch to pitch as many innings as he can, and then go with our regular bullpen. We have not been hitting, and in order to win this game, we've got to score runs or shut the Nationals out until we do," the coach explained.

The decision to start off with Tommy Levin shocked most of the team. Not once during the regular season had Coach Kessler started a reliever. Billy wondered if this was a strategic move to upset the Nat's the same way he had done against Slo-Mo. The more Billy thought about the coach's strategy, the more he liked it. He knew it could throw the Nationals off, just enough to eke out a win.

Game time came, and this game no different than the other World Series games. The players were introduced one by one on the baselines, and then the National Anthem. Billy was first up as the Royals were the visiting team. On the first pitch, he hit a long fly ball that bounced off the right field fence and slid into second base before the throw came in. Mack followed with a sacrifice bunt down the third base line, where the only thing the third baseman could do was throw to first for the out. But, it allowed Billy to advance to third base. With only one out, he could score even on a short fly ball to the outfield. Auturo was not thinking about a fly ball; he wanted a hit. On the second pitch, he hit a lazy flyball to centerfield. Billy knew it would be close. His metal spikes turning up the dirt behind him on the basepath. He reached the plate at the same time as the ball and was pretty sure he was safe. The umpire's arm went up in the air, signaling that Billy was out. "No way," Billy shouted. He got up and walked back to the umpire pleading his case, and at the same time, telling the umpire he'd blown that call. If Billy had argued another 10 seconds, he probably would have been thrown out of the game, but he was 90% sure he'd beaten the tag, even if the ball and Billy arrived at the same time. There was no way the catcher could have tagged Billy before he reached the plate because he had to turn around to tag him. The 47,000 in attendance were sure Billy was out, just like the umpire signaled, and they booed Billy as he walked slowly back to the dugout.

That was the third out of the inning, so now Coach Kessler's strategy would be seen by the Nat's. "A relief pitcher starting," they laughed. "Obviously, the Royals are feeling the heat, starting a relief pitcher," said one of the Nats players.

Tommy took to the mound. After his warm-up throws, he knelt behind the pitching mound like he was praying. Billy wondered if he was.

The first pitch was a 97 mph fastball on the outside corner. The ump yelled, "strike one." The fans booed again. The second pitch was a breaking ball that almost hit the plate, but the batter swung and missed. The count was now 0-2. Billy just hoped

Tommy could get through two scoreless innings. The next pitch was a called third strike. Tommy was wasting no time. He proceeded to strike the next two batters out, throwing only a total of 10 pitches, just like he'd done all year as a reliever.

The team reached the dugout cheering wildly for Tommy but did not score themselves in the second inning, and before they knew it, Tommy was back on the mound.

He didn't let up. For the first time all year, he struck out six straight hitters. The team was amazed. Coach Kessler was wondering if he should change his strategy of only pitching Tommy two innings. As the Royals batted, the coach was mulling over what he should do.

Art was starting in RF tonight, replacing Terrace, who normally batted fifth. Art made the Coach's strategy look good as he singled to left field. Jackson immediately laid down a perfect sacrifice bunt that got Art to second. Now it was up to Aaron. He took two pitches that were balls, one on the inside and one on the outside and high. The third pitch was what he was waiting for, a strike over the heart of the plate. He drilled a shot into the gap between the left and center fielder. Art scored easily on Aaron's double, so the Royals drew first blood and were now up 1-0. Then Coach Kessler surprised everyone again by bringing in a left-handed hitter, Don Wood, replacing the right-handed hitter, Jon Hahara. It was only the second inning, and the coach was pulling moves out that were not normal for him, but it paid off as Don hit a long fly ball that got up into the wind current, and the ball sailed over the right field fence. The Royals were up 3-0 in just the second inning.

Coach Kessler decided to stick to his original plan and bring in his normal starter, Butch Kelly, who had started the first game of the series. Kelly immediately threw four innings of no-hit ball, and the Nats never were able to start a rally, and before anyone knew it, the series was now tied, two games apiece, meaning that no matter who won the 5th game, the series would go back to Kansas City. If the Royals won the 5th game, they would only have to win one game in Kansas City, but if the Nats won, the Royals would have to win two games in KC.

Coach Kessler had his mind made up long before game time. It was time for Jim Strickland to start.

By game time, Billy was feeling good about the Royals winning. When he stepped into the batter's box facing a pitcher he'd only read about, Todd Cohen. Cohen had been with the Nats all year but had not had a good year as his ERA was 5.32. Billy knew last year, Cohen was one of the best pitchers in the National League. But this year, he just had not been able to match his stats of the year before.

Billy watched him warm-up, and he threw all fastballs. Billy was expecting a fastball on the first pitch to him. He guessed wrong as Cohen threw a curve that dipped down and hit the dirt behind the plate. Thankfully, Bill let it go by without swinging. "Ball One" signaled the ump. The young shortstop was ready for a fastball now. He watched the rotation on the ball and knew it was another curve. Again, he didn't swing, but this time, the ump called out loud, "Strike One." Billy decided not to even try to guess on the next pitch.....he just had to keep his eye on the ball until it hit his bat. He saw it was a fastball, and the crack of the bat said, "this ball is going a long way." It did as it flew over the centerfielder's head. Billy was running full steam even though he thought it was going to be a HR. The ball hit the base of the centerfield fence as Billy was already around first base. He kept running at top speed, now believing he had a triple as he crossed second base. As he looked over to the third base coach, he saw his arms up in the arm, meaning stop at 2nd base. The Nats knew Billy could not get a triple in the Nats ballpark and threw the ball to second base. Billy scrambled to get back to the bag before they tagged him out. He stumbled, and the ball was waiting for him as he finally got back to the base. "Yrrrr Out," yelled the umpire.

Mack and Ortero stuck out, ending the top of the first. Jim Strickland took to the mound, knowing he had to be sharp to keep the Nats from scoring. On his first pitch, the Nats leadoff batter hit a sharp ground ball to Billy's right. He backhanded it, planted his feet, and threw a strike to Bobby at first base. One out now and Billy thought, "OK, only 26 more outs."

Strickland got out of the inning with a scratch single and nothing else. No runs scored until Billy got up again. This time, in the top of the 4th, he hit the first pitch he saw, which was a fastball over the plate. He watched the ball hit the meat of his bat, and he knew he'd hit it hard again. Once again, he felt he had a HR, but after the last time up, he was taking no chances. He watched the ball hit the top of the fence and bounce over it, but he had no idea if it would be ruled a HR or a double, so he ran as fast as he could before seeing the umpire waving his hands above his head in a circle indicating it was a homerun. Billy slowed down and trotted around the bases. Most of the team was waiting for him between the dugout and the plate, all giving him high-fives and cheering "way to go, Billy."

Strickland was still pitching in the bottom of the 6th and had not allowed a run. The first batter hit a bloop single over Mack's head. No one could reach it, but Mack was fast enough that he got to the ball before any of the Outfielders, preventing the hitter from reaching second base. The pitching coach walked slowly to the mound. No one was warming up in the bullpen; thanks to the two-hit game, Jim was pitching. Everyone gathered around the pitching mound. The trip to the mound by the pitching coach was not to say anything to Strickland. Instead, he was there to talk to the infielders about who was going to cover the bag in the case of a steal, and telling them, "we need a double play here." He walked back to the dugout, and before he was seated, the next batter hit a sharp ground ball to Mack, who fielded it cleanly and threw a strike to Billy. He rifled the ball to Bobby at 1B, and now there were two outs and no one on base. The next batter hit a popup to Bobby, and the game was now going into the top of the 7th with the Royals holding on to their one run lead, Billy's homerun.

Art lead off with a single, and Coach Kessler immediately had Terrace run for Art because of the speed difference. Jackson hit a hard ground ball between the shortstop and the second baseman. The shortstop picked it up and backhanded the ball to the second baseman, who fired to 1B for a double play. Even Billy had to smile at that play.

Coach Kessler pulled another one of his unusual managing moves, bringing in the starter from the first game, and reliever in the last game, Butch Kelly. It took about a full minute before the move proved to not work as Pepper Gapper hit one over the left-field fence to tie the game. Coach Kessler was having two relievers warming up immediately, but before they barely started throwing, and Nat McConnell followed Gapper with another home run, giving the Nats a 2-1 lead.

Coach Kessler changed pitchers immediately, but it was too late as the Nats rolled to a win in the 5th game of the series. That meant the Royals had to win two straight at the "K" when they returned. The team got on the plane to return home. Billy sat next to Butch, who was hanging his head in his hands as the plane took off for KC.

"Butch, do not let this game get to you," encouraged Billy. "We have to win two games at home in order to win the World Series, meaning you will pitch again before the series is over, so do not let this get to you."

The plane landed in KC, and by then, Butch was laughing. Billy had done all he could to pump some encouragement back into the pitcher.

# <u>30</u>

## Back Home In KC

The plane landed at 4:00 AM. The team finally got to the Hyatt close to 5:00 AM. They were tired. The rest of the day was an off day, so no one was up before noon. Billy woke up at about 12:45 PM. He ordered breakfast to his room, which was a special perk for the team staying at Hyatt's in each city during the season. There were many perks, but breakfast at 1:00 was Billy's favorite.

After eating, Billy called his folks, who had anxiously been waiting to hear from him. "So are you exhausted yet, Billy?' his dad asked, laughing. "You have no idea, Dad. I had no clue the energy required for the play-offs and then the World Series," Billy confessed to his dad. "We've already played 171 games," Billy continued. The energy required the past month has been unreal. Every pitch is almost like a game itself," he laughed, trying to explain to his dad what the team had gone through.

"We've got about an hour of loosing up this afternoon, in fact, in about an hour," Billy started his thought. "As soon as it's over, I'm coming home. Is Emma there?"

"Of course. She's been here for each game. She's going to school at KU, which is only about 30 minutes from us, so we've known, if there was a game that day, she was going to be here," his dad told his son.

Billy got an Uber and had all sorts of thoughts on the ride to his Lenexa home. He wondered how

Emma was doing at KU in her classes. He wondered how his folks were doing. He wondered how Mr. Booker was doing. At the same time, his main thought broke in, wondering about the last game or two at the "K," knowing the Royals had to win two straight games. One loss and the Royals would finish number two.

Arriving at his home, Emma came running out, jumping into Billy's arms. Then she kissed him right in front of his folks. He was a little embarrassed, but it made no difference. It was so good seeing her. Then his Dad broke in, saying, "Hey Emma, let us hug Billy.' Emma laughed and let Mr. Tankersly hug his son. Billy's Mom broke in and gave him the biggest hug of all. "It was good to be home," Billy thought.

As they sat around in the living room, all of them were throwing questions at him. "How many steals do you have?" was the first question from his Dad. "I finished the regular season with 89, missing my goal of 100, which was what Ricky had his first full year," Billy answered. "In the playoffs and World Series, I've only had 12 steals, so my production has gone down," Billy frowned.

Emma spoke. "So you now have 102 steals," she stated. "You've done it, Billy," she exclaimed.

"Not the same," Billy threw out. "But who knows, I might get three or four in the next two games," he laughed.

Just talking about the upcoming game or games made Billy realize he needed to get back to the Hyatt where he could be focused on the game tomorrow.

"Dad, can I borrow your car for about 30 minutes....I want to go see Mr. Booker," Billy explained. Naturally, his dad handed him the keys, and Billy hugged Emma goodbye as he walked out the door.

"Well, look at who's my door. The American League's rookie of the year," Mr. Booker said as he hugged Billy.

"How are you doing, Mr. Booker?" Billy asked.

"I'm doing much better, Billy. Thanks for asking," Mr. Booker replied. Then he asked, "How are you doing?"

Billy smiled and told his mentor that he had no idea how much energy major leaguers put out. Mr. Booker laughed, saying, "Groundskeeper's work twice as hard as you, young man." Billy laughed.

It was a good 30 minutes with Mr. Booker. As he headed back home, he knew he'd have to tell them he couldn't stay very long.

"Dad, Mom, Emma....I have to get back to the hotel to have my mind on the game tomorrow," Billy told them. "What if I drive you to the hotel, Billy?" Emma asked. "That would be great, and 15 minutes later, after hugging his Dad and Mom, Billy was headed back to the Hyatt.

"Billy, you have had a good season, but the next two games are the most important of your life. You have to win these two games. No one will remember who finished second. They will remember the champions as long as baseball goes on," Emma encouraged him.

"For sure, Em," Billy replied. He was already picturing standing on the winner's stand accepting the most valuable player award. Billy thought that would be possible if he had a great last two games.

"Em, count on us winning, and either me or Bobby being selected the MVP," Billy said, matter of factly.

"Geezzzz, I guess I didn't have to encourage you, Mr. Stolen Base King," she replied. "You aren't lacking confidence, that's for sure."

"Em, in baseball, you have to believe what you can't see for it to happen the way you want," Billy said. He went on, "one thing I've truly learned in playing baseball is what Jesus said in the Book of Mark. Jesus told us we could have anything if we believe we've already received it. So, I believe we are going to win the World Series no matter what the odds are against us," Billy said confidently.

"Well, I guess you have a new name now, Billy. You are King of the Scriptures......except for one thing. You only quoted part of what Jesus said. He also told us, even if we believe we've already received it, it won't happen if we don't forgive everyone for everything we've held against them," Emma said to Billy.

"Wow, Em, I didn't want to sound like a preacher, or I would have said that.....I know it for sure. Every night, when I'm praying, I start by forgiving everyone for anything that happened during the day, even the stupid driver that just cut in front of us," he laughed out loud. "I am happy that you are reading the Bible, too, Em. We are a lot alike. I like that a lot," Billy smiled as they caught each other's glance.

"Billy, we're almost to the "K." I just want you to know I'm right there by your side, and I have no doubt, the Royals are going to win these two games, and you are going to be MVP," Emma said in a serious vein.

She kissed Billy with a good luck kiss as he got out of the car and headed into the hotel. His baseball juices were already flowing.

Bobby was the first person he saw. "Well, here we are, Mr. Stolen Base champion. The final two games of the World Series, just like we imagined so many years ago. What fun, Billy," Bobby smiled. It was a cocky smile like he knew they were going to win both games.

The team had a short infield session that afternoon to warm them up for the game the next day. Then they each had five minutes in the batting cage. All the players were back in the clubhouse two hours later.

"What a time to remember," Mack said to Billy, with excitement in his voice. Everyone was pumped. It seemed they all knew they were going to win the next two games, now that they were back at the "K." The fans alone would make the difference.

Everyone ate together at Joe's Barbeque and were back in their rooms by 9:00 PM. Billy was in bed by 10:00 PM with his bat right next to him. As he was drifting off to sleep, he had a thought. "I need to name my bat." With that, Billy was sound asleep.

# 31

## Time To Shine

"What a feeling," Billy thought as he was taking batting practice, and the stands were already nearly filled.  He could hear many of the fans calling out his name.  Even though Billy was the youngest on either team, he knew it was time for him to shine.

In the clubhouse, Coach Kessler told the team that Farmer Hart was pitching the 6th game of the series for the Royals.  "Guys, all of you know, this is a must-win game for us.  Farmer, I'll be watching every pitch, and if I see something that is not looking right, I'll have no choice but to bring in our relievers.  Farmer nodded in understanding and gave the coach a thumbs up. Butch and Maverick, be ready at any point to come in.  We will do everything to win this game....we have to," the Coach said.

Billy was a little surprised that he might be using Butch out of the pen because he'd been the starting pitcher in the first game.  He thought about it and decided the coach was going to do anything in his power to win this one game.  Right now, it was a one-game series.

The game started with the usual fanfare before each of the games.  To Billy, it seemed to take forever.  Finally, the umpire yelled, "Play Ball."

Farmer was sharp from the first pitch, a sweeping curve that caught the corner of the plate.  The umpire's arm went up, indicating it was strike one. Billy was always happy to see his team's pitcher start off with a strike.  On the next pitch,  a hard hit ball was out of the reach of the third baseman, but Billy was diving to his right, and from his knees, he threw to Bobby at 1B. The throw was a little short, but Bobby scooped it up with no problem, and the Royals had their first out. Farmer struck out the next two National players, including Pepper Gapper.

Billy swung the heavy bat in the on deck circle while Grant Bubble warmed up. Billy had faced Bubble in the first game. He remembered getting his first stolen base off the National's pitcher his first time up. He intended to get on, one way or another, and do the same this game.

Once again, the Nat's infield was playing Billy like a pull hitter with the second baseman in short right field and with the third baseman on the first base side of second base. The shortstop was responsible for the entire third base side of the diamond. There was no doubt in Billy's mind; he was going to bunt down the third baseline. There was no way the shortstop could get to the ball in time to throw him out. Before the pitch, he wondered why in the world they were giving him first base. They had to know he would take advantage of their shift and hit to left, or bunt.

They were just being deceptive. Even before Billy squared to lay a bunt down, the shortstop was racing in toward where he expected Billy to bunt. Billy saw him, but it was too late. The bunt was perfect as it was down the third-base line and just died about halfway. Bubble, the pitcher, tried to get to it. The shortstop tried, but there was no way they were going to get the speedster, Billy Tankersly. He crossed first base a good ½ second before the ball arrived.

The Kansas City fans yelled loudly. Kansas City was a baseball town, where the fans knew almost as much about the game as the players. All 47,000 fans knew Billy would steal second on the first or second pitch. Billy watched Bubble like a hawk. He watched every movement Bubble made. He led off enough to try to catch the signal the catcher was giving Bubble. He thought he saw that it might be a pitch-out, so he stayed close to the bag. Sure enough, the catcher had called a pitch out to the first pitch to Mack. Billy looked in and smiled at Mack, who never took the bat off his shoulder.

Mack was not going to swing until Billy was at 2B, or he had two strikes on him. The next pitch was a fastball right in the middle of the plate. Mack had a hard time laying off it. But Billy was safe at second after one more stolen base, and now Mack had a man to drive in. Two more fastballs that Mack took for balls. The count was now 3-1, and Mack expected a good pitch to hit. It didn't come as he trotted down to first base with a walk. Now the Royals had their first two men on, with no outs. Auturo stepped into the batter's box, knowing full well that Coach Kessler might signal a double steal. Bubble walked around the mound, picked up the rosin bag, looked at the ball, and ran his hands over it like it was his best friend. And right now, he needed a best friend as the Royals were in a good position to score first, and that was the last thing Bubble wanted. He got his sign from the catcher, and for some lapse of memory or trying something different, he never looked back to second base. Billy and Mack were both off running, and both were safe as the catcher never even bothered to throw it to either base. Seeing the entire field through his catcher's mask, he saw Bubble not even look back to second, and Billy and Mack, both with big leads, were sure to steal 2nd and 3rd.

Auturo now had men on second base and third base. A base hit would score both. Everyone on the team was standing in the dugout cheering Auturo on. A two-run lead in the first inning would have the fans in a frantic mood, cheering wildly and waving their blue towels. Billy learned later that it was a standing-room only crowd, and they were so loud, the third base coach said something to Billy, and he could not understand him. Thankfully, Auturo hit one up against the left field fence, with both runners scoring.

Several years ago, a company ran tests in each pro football team to see who had the loudest crowd. That was at Arrowhead, the Chiefs football stadium, right next door to the "K" had the loudest crowd among all professional football teams. As Mack crossed the plate, Billy was sure this KC crowd was louder than the KC crowd at Arrowhead. It was a madhouse with people still standing as
Bobby came up.

Bubble was visibly shaken. The Royals had the lead in the first inning, and he was not comfortable with this much noise, and having the first two batters score before he could even get an out. He knew Bobby was the power hitter on the team, and with Autruo on second base, Bubble had to make sure he got Bobby out. That turned out to be wishful thinking as Bobby hit one over the centerfield fence on the first pitch to him. The Royals now led 4-0 with no outs in the first inning.

The Nationals manager strolled to the mound. What could he possibly say to his best pitcher after seeing the first four batters scoring, with no outs? The crowd was so loud; Billy wondered if Bubble could hear him anyway. Terrance and Jackson both walked. Six batters had come to the plate, and six batters had reached base. Once again, the National's manager walked slowly to the mound. This time, with no hesitation, he waved his left arm in the air, meaning that Josh Harkins, who the Royals had not seen in the entire series, was coming in to try to stop the bleeding. Art Holmes was now up with a chance to add more runs. On the first pitch to Art, he blasted one into the right field corner, driving in another two runs. No outs, six runs, and a man on second. All Billy could do was smile. The energy in the dugout was palpable. No one was sitting.

The rest of the game was anti-climatic as the Royals won 8-2 and were headed toward game seven in the World Series. In the clubhouse after the game, there was no cheering, just everyone talking about game seven and potential Champions of the World with one more victory. Billy had two hits, stole three bases, and scored three runs, plus making a tremendous play behind second base, flipping to Mack at 2B from his glove. It was a game where everyone had performed perfectly for the Royals.

There were a lot of smiles as the team ate dinner in a private room at the Hyatt, but no one was not celebrating. Everyone knew the Royals had to win one more game.

<h1 style="text-align:center"><u>32</u></h1>

## It All Comes Down To This

The entire season had come down to one game.  As Billy and Bobby sat in the dugout together during batting practice, they talked about their careers leading up to this one game.  They talked about their Little League championship so many years ago, and neither had forgotten.

"If we still remember that game, like it was yesterday, I wonder how long we will remember this game," Billy commented.  "Probably forever, Billy," Bobby smiled.  "This has been our dream since we were nine years old.  "But, we have to win it," Billy said to his best friend.  Bobby replied, "We will."

Game time approached, and the grandstands were a solid blue with every Royals fan wearing clothing that made the entire stadium look blue.

The announcers were almost as excited as the Royals and Nationals.  "Tim, this has been one of those Championship series no one will ever forget."  "Jim, it's one we'll never forget, that's for sure.  The media guide is one we may keep forever," said Jim Borrows, the voice of every major championship in sports for ten years.  "What do you think about this kid from Kansas City, Billy Tankersly?" Borrows asked his co-announcer.  "Oh my gosh, this kid is exciting to watch, both at the plate and in the field.  He's hitting .310 in the playoffs and World Series and has 16 stolen bases plus five or six plays at short that very few shortstops could have made.  Overall, right now, he has 105 stolen bases for the season, and that is in Ricky Henderson's territory," Tom Boyce raved.

Borrows added, "that is why this media guide is one we may never part with. No matter who wins the game, the guide says it all when it describes Tankersly as a player everyone wants to see.  He brings so much excitement to every game. Personally, from everything I've read all year about the kid, I think he has a good shot at breaking Ricky's record of 1407 stolen bases, a record that no one ever expected to be broken," added Jim Borrows.

The fans were cheering wildly long before the game started.  The Royals had not won a World Series in 50 years, so this was a day the fans would remember forever, especially if the Royals won.

After the pre-game ceremonies, the Royals took the field with the fans screaming, "Let's go Royals, Let's go Royals."  It was a memory Billy wanted to hold on to just like he had when he stepped to the plate in Lexington in his first professional baseball game.  Then, like now, he looked from the left field stands to the right field stands. "What a feeling," he thought to himself.

Pitching for the Royals was Butch Kelly, who had started one game and then came in as a reliever in another.  Coach Kessler had a great deal of faith in Butch. He only took three warmup pitches, which shocked the Nationals. No starting pitcher only took three warmup pitches.

But Kelly knew what he was doing.  He wanted to pitch the entire nine innings and was wasting no more energy than he had to.

Butch struck out the first two Nationals he faced. Then stepping into the batter's box was Pepper

Gapper, who led all the major leagues with 53 HR's during the season, and two more in the playoffs and series. Kelly got the sign from the catcher and immediately threw a curve that bounced off the plate....and Gapper swung at it. When Butch was at his best, no one could hit him. Gapper took the next pitch for a called strike and then hit a weak ground ball to Billy. It was so slow getting to him; he had to charge it, picked it up with one hand, and threw to Bobby off balance. Bobby stretched as far as he could, and everyone knew Gapper was out. Everyone except the first base umpire who called him safe. Coach Kessler looked at the video that every major league manager had and put his hands to his ears that meant he wanted to challenge the call. The umpires huddled while one talked to the New York office, who had the final say on the play. They had cameras showing many different angles, and within a minute, they were back on the field, raising their arms to indicate Gapper was out.

The fans were as loud as Billy had ever experienced at any game. The noise was deafening as Billy stepped into the batter's box.

Billy had his mind made up on what he was going to do. He was going to take the first pitch, no matter whether it was a strike or ball. "Ball One," yelled the umpire. He had to yell for anyone to know he'd called it a Ball.

That put more pressure on the Nationals pitcher Steve Clark, normally a middle reliever, but both coaches were pulling all sorts of tricks out of the bag. In Billy's mind, Clark had to throw a strike now. He did, and Billy swung hard. He missed it. Now it was even between the batter and pitcher.

Neither had an advantage. Both the pitcher and Billy thought the count was in their favor, even though it was 1-1.

Billy remembered his game against "Slo-Mo," where he stepped out on each pitch, putting more pressure on the pitcher. So, he stepped out, once Clark had his sign from the catcher. That meant the pitcher and catcher had to go through the signs all over again. Once again, Clark got his signs, and Billy stepped out of the box. Billy saw a look on the pitcher's face that said, "Come on, stay in the box." He felt the advantage was definitely on his side now.

The pitch came in, and Billy let it go by as a ball. Now the count was 2-1 with the odds favoring the batter. Billy was ready to hit the next pitch, no matter whether it was a curve, fastball, or cutter. If it was on the outside, Billy was going to hit to left. If it was over the plate or even a little inside, he was going to pull the ball. It was on the inside, and Billy swung with power. He was not sure if it would be caught in deep right field, go over the fence for a HR, or curve foul. Either way, he ran.

In the TV booth, the announcers could see right away. "The speedster Tankersly is going to get a double on that one," said John Benson, the play by play announcer said into the microphone."

Billy wasn't watching the ball. He was running, rounding first like it wasn't even there. On the way to second base, he could hear the crowd. They were moaning. "Not a good sign," thought Billy as he approached second base, looking to the third base coach to see if he should try for a triple. The coach was bent over with his hands on his knees. At that point, Billy knew the right fielder had caught up with the ball and made the catch.  Even though he hadn't seen the catch, he figured it had to be a great one.

John Benson, in a higher than usual voice, described the play, "My gosh, Richter got to that ball and caught it right before it went over the fence. Tankersly was robbed of a home run," he continued.

Billy walked back to the dugout, looking to right field and wondering how Richter was able to catch up with the ball.  He saw their pitcher tipping his hat.  "It must have been a good play," thought Billy.

From that point on, Clark was perfect, neither allowing a hit or a walk through the first five innings. Billy had hit a hard ground ball to the second baseman in the last of the 4th and was easily thrown out.

Kelly had given up one hit and no bases on balls through the 5th.  It was indeed a pitcher's game with the score 0-0 in the top of the 6th.  Kelly retired the Nats one, two, three in the top of the 6th.

One of the bottom three hitters had to get on base for Billy to get up.  Terrace was batting 7th, Art Hart 8th, and Tommy Robinson, tonight's catcher, 9th in Coach Keller's lineup, again trying to do anything to throw off the Nat's.  Terrace struck out.  Now Art or Tommy had to get on for Billy to get up to bat.  Art took the count to 3&2 and watched the next pitch outside for a base on balls.  One out now and Tommy stepped into the box, with Billy in the on deck circle.

Tommy wasted no time.  On the first pitch, he hit a ground ball that darted between the 3B and the SS for the first hit of the game for the Royals, but Art had to hold up at 2B.  With men on 1st and 2nd, Billy had a chance to put the Royals in the lead.  The Nationals manager walked to the mound, briskly, waving his left arm in the air. Billy didn't recognize the pitcher coming in. He walked back to the dugout while this reliever warmed up, asking, "Who is this guy?" Coach Keller said, "he's a rookie that came up in September and has not allowed a run since being called up. I'm sure they've saved him for this one outing."

Billy watched him in his last warm-up pitch. It was a curve, so Billy understood right away that he had more than just a fastball.

"Let's go Royals, Let's go Royals," screamed the KC fans. Everyone was standing, waving blue towels that were given out each game of the series, played in KC. Billy knew a single would get Art in, giving the Royals the lead.

The 19-year-old shortstop stepped into the box, looking over the field, seeing where the Nationals were playing him in this situation. The shift was not on. The infielders were at their normal slots, and the outfielders were playing in a bit, hoping to cut down Art at the plate if Billy hit a ground ball that got through the infield.

"Strike One," indicated the ump on the first pitch. Billy had a good eye, and he did not think the ball was even close to the plate. He turned and said something to the umpire. Then came one of those moments in a game that can turn it around completely. The umpire, Bill Brown, took a step toward Billy, telling him to "cool it." The KC fans were afraid Billy was going to be thrown out of the game, the way he was acting. He was making it clear he disagreed with the umpire's call. Coach Kessler walked out, getting between the umpire and Billy, telling Billy to "stop it." He then turned to Brown and had his own words with him.  Before Billy realized it, Brown was throwing Coach Kessler out of the game.  The argument went on for another minute.  Finally, the coach headed to the clubhouse, able to watch the rest of the game on TV, but not able to manage.

Even though it was not what anyone on the Royals wanted, it did cause enough commotion that the pitcher threw his second pitch about a foot over Billy's head.  On the next pitch, Billy hit a hard line-drive over 2nd base. It was a single, and Art was trying to score.  Billy had already crossed first base as he saw the home plate umpire's arms out, indicating Art was safe and the Royals led, 1-0 in the 6th.  Tommy had gone to third base since the throw went to the plate.

Now the Royals had a man on first and third, with two outs, and Mack up.  Mack knew Billy would attempt to steal second base on the first pitch.  Sure enough, Billy took off the moment the pitcher's leg went over the rubber.  The catcher faked a throw to second base and threw to third base, trying to get Tommy napping. Tommy had not moved from his lead off position and was back to the base easily. Now the Royals had runners at second and third, with Mack up.  A single would give the Royals a two-run lead if Billy got a good jump off second base. Sure enough, Mack hit a ground ball over the second base bag. Tommy scored easily, and Billy was glad to see his coach waving him to the plate.  The throw came in as Billy slid across the plate safely, giving the Royals a 3-0 lead.

Arturo hit a fly ball to left for the third out. Going into the top of the 7th, the Kansas City fans were envisioning a World Series championship. The acting manager, Hortenz Winston, made up his mind, he would let Kelly face one batter at a time, but if anyone got on, he had Jim Strickland warmed up in the bullpen. The first Nat's hitter got on, and Peter Gapper was the next batter. Coach Winston walked to the mound, waving his right arm in the air, indicating he wanted Strickland. The fans cheered Butch Kelly as he walked off the field with a three-run lead in the 7th game of the World Series.

Gapper came up with a man on first base, and on the first pitch from Strickland, Gapper hit one of the longest balls ever hit at the "K." It cleared the fountains in centerfield. With one pitch, the Nationals were back in the game, trailing by one run. The next batter singled, and out came Coach Winston. He talked to Strickland for a long time before the umpire came out to break up the meeting on the mound. Just then, Coach Winston raised his arm for the left-handed Charlie Triller, who was another of the September call ups. Triller had played at Omaha most of the year and had a sterling 0.98 ERA for the Storm Chasers.

Triller took his warm-up pitches and was ready to face Victor Though, who had two HR's in the playoffs and World Series. He had the power to put the Nationals in the lead. Triller checked the man on first and threw a perfect meatball to Though. He swung like he was going for a HR. He missed it. Billy wiped the sweat off his forehead because he felt the ball was going to leave the park, but instead it was Strike One. Triller checked the runner at 1B and threw a curve that was his "get 'em out" pitch. Though let it go by. The umpire raised his arm in the air, and Through was by the umpire's side before anyone realized it. He was arguing more than Billy had. The Nat's Manager ran out, separating Though from the umpire. He had a few words with Brown, the umpire, but did not get thrown out. The KC fans booed, and to Billy, it sounded like a freight train colliding with another freight train. The boo birds were loud.

Triller now had the advantage with the count being 0-2. He shook off two signs before finally nodding his head up and down. From the shortstop position, Billy could see the sign. It was the same pitch that Triller shook off initially. Billy knew that Triller shaking off two pitches, and going with the first sign, he was trying to win the mental advantage over the hitter. The pitch was a fastball on the inside of the plate. Though hit a bullet through the infield that Mack had no chance of getting. The runner on first rounded second base and was waved on to third base. The throw went to second, keeping the potential lead run at 1B. But the Nats now had runners at 1st and 3rd, trailing by one run with no outs. The KC crowd was quiet for the first time in the series. With the tying run at 3B, a fly ball could tie the game up.

Coach Winston walked to the mound again. This was the 7th game of the World Series. The winner would be the National Champions, and right now, the Royals lead was in jeopardy. Coach Winston talked to Thiller and the infielders for a couple of minutes. He instructed the infielder to come in and on a ground ball, be prepared to throw to the plate to get the runner if he tried to score.

Billy knew with no outs, it was pointless to try to get a double play because the runner at third base would tie the game if he scored. They had to get him out if he tried to advance.

The hitter took two pitches for balls. The tension in the grandstands could be felt two miles away. On the third pitch, he hit a ground ball directly at Billy, but the runner was not trying to score. Billy knew if he threw to 1B, that runner would advance to second base and represent the tie-breaking run. Instead of throwing to 1B, Billy did something unheard of in baseball. He started running to second base, while all the time looking at the runner on third. It was a gamble. He was able to tag the runner, while still looking at 3B, and threw a no-look strike to Bobby at 1B for a double play with the runner still at 3B.

The announcers were talking about what looked like it was going to be a tie game when Billy pulled some magic out of his hat. "Holy Smokes, did you see that play?" the play by play announcer shouted into the microphone. 'I've never seen anything like that. You know what allowed that play to happen?" he asked. Without waiting for an answer, he continued. "Tankersly's speed. No other Shortstop in the game could have made that play!"

The game was still 3-2 with the Royals leading, but the tying run was on third. He was so surprised by Tankersly's play that he didn't even try to score. It didn't matter as the next hitter drilled a line drive off the left field fence for a double, driving in the tying run. It was now 3-3 with a runner for the Nats on second base.

The announcers were still shocked by Billy's play on the last batter. "You know, if Tankersly had not made that play, the Nationals would be in the lead right now. By him tagging the runner as he came into second base, it prevented another run from scoring. "But here we sit in the 7th game of the World Series, all tied up in the top of the 7th inning," said the same announcer who was raving about Billy's play. "But, the lead run for the Nationals is on second base, and it could be a great comeback if they can take the lead."

Coach Winston walked to the mound with his mind made up. He was bringing in Farmer Hart, who started the game yesterday. Billy thought that it was really strange since Farmer started yesterday, but Billy had confidence in Farmer. He wondered if Coach Kessler would have made the same decision.

On the first pitch, the batter hit a hard ground ball to Billy's right. He was hoping the third baseman could get it, but he didn't, and Billy picked up the grounder and off-balance, he threw to Bobby at first base. Bobby made a fantastic play by stretching even though it appeared the ball was not going to reach him in time as it bounced before Bobby could scoop it up. It was a bang-bang play at 1B, and the umpire raised his arm in the air, yelling, "Yrrrr out."

The Nationals manager came running out to the home plate umpire, making sure he knew the Nationals were going to challenge that play. The umpires gathered by the batter's box on the Royals side. Billy and the rest of the team were already in the dugout.

After almost two minutes, the umpires broke their huddle, and the head umpire raised his arm in the air meaning the play stood. The Nationals had tied the game though, 3-3.

Bobby was up first for the Royals. The grandstands were loud again, shouting, "Let's go Royals, Let's go Royals."

On the third pitch, Bobby hit a long, long fly ball to centerfield. Could the centerfielder reach it in time? The only way he could have reached it would have been if he had an arm 20 feet long because Bobby had untied the game with his 4th HR during the playoffs and World Series. The entire team greeted Bobby at the plate, cheering wildly. Terrace followed with a single. Jackson was going to face a reliever for the Nationals as the manager was on the mound before Terrace reached first base. Jackson laid down a perfect sacrifice bunt, moving Terrace to second base. Art Hart was up next, and a single would give the Royals a two-run lead. After working the count to 2-2, Art swung at a pitch that dropped so fast, it hit the plate, and the catcher held on to it as the umpire raised his right arm in the air, indicating Art was out. Two outs now, and Terry, the catcher, was up. He struck out on three pitches, so the Royals led by one run going into the top of the 8th inning.

The coach allowed Farmer to start the inning. With two outs, the Nationals finally got a man on first base. Billy wondered what Coach Winston would do now. The coach was happy with Farmer and left him in to get the final out in the 8th inning. It was a good decision as the Nats hitter hit a slow ground ball to Mack, who picked it up barehanded and flipped the ball to Bobby for the third out.

Now in the bottom of the 8th, Billy was second up. Coach Winston brought Tommy David in to pinch hit. On the first pitch, he hit a ground ball to the pitcher who tossed it to the first baseman for out number one. Billy stepped into the box determined to get on base; however he could. He took the first two pitches, but the second pitch was called a strike. So, with a 1-1 count, Billy dropped a drag bunt down the first baseline. It was placed perfectly between the first baseman and the second baseman. The pitcher was the only one who could reach it, but because the first baseman had gone for the ball, there was no one covering first as Billy crossed the bag.

Here in the bottom of the 8th of a 3-3 7th game of the World Series, the Royals had the tie-breaking runner on first base, and it was their speedy shortstop, who everyone watching in the grandstands and on TV knew Billy Tankersly was going to steal second base. Mack took the first pitch for a ball. It wasn't a pitchout but was far enough outside; there was no way Mack could have hit it if he'd wanted to do so.

The second pitch was the same. Far outside. Yet, Billy did not even attempt to get a jump. His Dad, looking from the grandstands, wondered if his son had been hurt. All season long, Billy would have been at 2B after two pitches to Mack.

Mack had the count in his favor. Two balls and no strikes. Would Billy try to steal here? "Ball Three" said the ump over the sound of the crowd, all waiting for Billy to steal. The Nats pitcher was in a major hole. He had to throw a strike or risk walking

Mack, putting a man on first and second.  Again, Billy had not made an attempt to steal.  On the 4th pitch, Billy acted like he was going, but stayed put at 1B.  The pitch was a strike over the heart of the plate.  Nothing changed as far as the pitcher not having room to be fancy with a cutter or curve.  He had to throw a strike over the heart of the plate, or he'd have a man on first and second.

As expected, the pitch was over the center of the plate.  Mack could wait no longer.  He swung and hit a line drive that dropped right in front of the left fielder.   Billy couldn't advance any further than second base as the left fielder was playing in, but now the Royals had runners at 1B and 2B with only one out.  Auturo stepped into the batter box, hoping to get a hit to score Billy from second base.

The Nats pitcher took a long time getting on the rubber, looking over his shoulder back at Tankersly.  Finally, he stepped on the rubber. He took a quick peek back at Billy, but not enough to keep Billy close to the bag, and that was all the shortstop needed.  He was on third base without a throw, and Mack, knowing, if Billy stole, his job was to be on the move as well.  Both runners moved up a base, and now the Nationals Manager walked to the mound.  He had a long talk with their pitcher but left him in, much to Billy and Mack's surprise.  While the manager was on the mound, time had been called.  Billy walked back toward second to talk to Mack. "Hey, Mr. Speed guy, why didn't you steal 2B….I sure gave  you every opportunity to do so." Mack said as he bent over to adjust his pants.  Billy didn't smile, he said matter of factly, "I would have, but their pitcher was keeping me close without throwing over," Billy explained to

Mack. "I wondered because I sort of figured you just wanted me to be the hero, rather than you this game," Mack laughed. "You know me well enough to know, Mack, I just want to win this game." Mack shook his head up and down as he walked back to 2B while Billy trotted over to 3B.

Arturo was in the box with Billy on 3B and Mack on 2nd with only one out. He knew if he could hit a fly ball any place in the outfield that Billy would score.

The first pitch was a strike on the inside corner. Arturo let it go by for a called strike. He stepped out, not taking his eyes off the pitcher. He figured since the first one had been called a strike, the next pitch would be a curve. He guessed right, but the ball dropped, hit in front of the plate, and then got by the catcher. Billy and Mack both took off.

The catcher got to the ball quickly. He turned to throw to the pitcher covering, but he wasn't there. Billy crossed the plate standing up with Mack moving up to third base. The crowd was going wild. Their hometown hero had done it one more time. The Royals had retaken the lead, 4-3 in the bottom of the 8th. The catcher walked to the mound, hearing his pitcher telling him that he screwed up. "Where was your head?" he said to the pitcher, loud enough for Billy to hear, even over the KC fans. He couldn't hear what the pitcher replied, but it wasn't important. The Royals led, and that was all Billy cared about.

The team bolted from the dugout, slapping Billy on the head, butt, and anyplace else they could slap him in appreciation. Arturo ended up taking a base on balls on a 3&2 count. Now the Royals had a man on 1st and 3rd with Bobby coming up with only one out. He knew, and everyone in the stadium knew if he just hit a long fly ball, Mack could get in from third base, giving the Royals a two-run cushion going into the top of the 9th.

On the first pitch, Bobby's bat had that "crack" noise that meant he'd hit it squarely. It wasn't only hit squarely, it was almost out of the Stadium, over the right field fence up into the concession area for a three-run homer, giving the Royals a 7-3 lead. The crowd was standing, stomping, clapping each other, and knowing that the Royals were going to win their first World Series in 50 years. Terrance and Jackson both hit fly balls that were caught, but it didn't make any difference. The team knew, for the first time in several long years, the Royals were going to have a parade down Main Street and up to the Union Station.

Josh Hamilton came in to close it out, and he did just that. The hearts of the Nationals were broken.

When the last out was made, the Royals all jumped out of the dugout to rush anyone they could find. They were celebrating in a big pile by the mound. They were World Series Champions!

# 33

## World Series Champions

No one had left the stadium. The fireworks were going off for a good five minutes, but they were not nearly as exciting as the 8th inning. Billy was being interviewed by a national TV color announcer over by the dugout. "Billy, why didn't you steal once you got on base?" the announcer asked him. "Well, first off because their pitcher was holding me on with eye glances," Billy answered. "Eye glances?" the announcer asked. "I know, after all my steals this year, you'd think in the biggest game I've ever played in, I'd go, but it's just not that easy," Billy laughed. "Well, you had no problem stealing home," the announcer laughed with Billy. "Was that called a steal?" Billy asked. "Yep, the official scorer gave you a steal." Billy was happy over not just winning the game, but knowing that was his 108th steal in his first season. "Ricky better watch out," he said to the announcer, who was a little puzzled initially until he realized, this young shortstop has a goal of breaking Ricky Henderson's stolen base record. He didn't say anything about what he'd realized but said, "Thanks, Billy, go celebrate with your team."

Billy went straight to Bobby, yelling, "We did it. Our dreams came true." Bobby hugged his best friend, yelling back at him, "Can you believe two nine-year old kids predicted this day?" They both laughed while jumping up and down.

Billy and Bobby both helped bring a World Series Championship to their hometown Kansas City

Royals, and Billy was on his way to breaking Ricky's record.

## The End

# Book IV

It was now two years since the Royals won the World Series.  The last two years, they finished second in the American League, and Billy had 80 stolen bases the year after the World Series win, and 102 in his third year with the Royals.  He now had a total of 290 stolen bases after three years.

He was still dating Emma, and she was in her final year at KU, in sports management.  They laughed together a lot, thinking that if the Royals hired her, Billy would have to be in her hands as far as his salary was concerned.  He wasn't too worried as he and Bobby had become heroes in Kansas City, with billboards all around the city.  They showed Billy Tankersly sliding into a base on one side, and Bobby Bonds game-seven homer on the other side, even two years after winning the World Series.

# About the Author

Warren Haskin grew up on the outskirts of Kansas City in Mission, Kansas. When he became a Cub Scout, his Dad and several other fathers obtained land at the edge of town to build a baseball diamond for their sons. It was truly the first Field of Dreams. From that moment on, Warren's dream was to be good enough to play major league ball.

He played college baseball in the Big 12 for the University of Kansas Jayhawks and for the Navy in a semi-pro league in Memphis, Tennessee, but his dream changed directions when he married. As a young husband and father of two, he embarked on a life-long career as an entrepreneur developing personal growth programs using much of what he'd learned from baseball.

Warren's passion for the sport has remained throughout his life. He has been a player, coach, sports editor, baseball and football announcer, business developer and owner, and trainer.

This is Warren's third fiction book. Like in Metal Spikes I and II, his inspirational teaching shows from the first to the last chapter through the "coaches," along the way, who teach young people and adults how to succeed.

He currently resides in Austin, Texas and is a business and personal consultant for Help People, Inc. He can be reached at whaskin@HelpPeople.com.